That
Doggone
Calf

D1366302

That Doggone Calf

Bill and Carol Wallace

Holiday House / New York

HOLIDAY HOUSE is registered in the U.S. Patent and Trademark Office.
Printed and bound in April, 2010 at Maple Vail, York, PA, USA.
www.holidayhouse.com
3   5   7   9   10   8   6   4   2

Library of Congress Cataloging-in-Publication Data

Wallace, Bill, 1947–
That doggone calf / by Bill and Carol Wallace. — 1st ed.
p. cm.
Summary: A new calf and a ranch's loyal herding dog disagree, but
eventually they learn to get along together.
ISBN 978-0-8234-2228-9 (hardcover)
ISBN 978-0-8234-2303-3 (paperback)
[1. Dogs—Fiction.   2. Cattle—Fiction.   3. Ranch life—Fiction.]
I. Wallace, Carol, 1948–   II. Title.
PZ7.W15473Th 2009
[Fic]—dc22
2009016201

To Ian Turpin

Chapter 1

The fall moon went to sleep someplace beyond the wheat field. The sun wasn't up yet, but the early morning light was more than enough for me to start my Daybreak Patrol. Trouble was, I didn't want to get up.

Between the coyotes coming too close to the house last night, the two raccoons trying to get into the sweet feed, and the opossum trying to steal our dry food, I didn't get that much sleep. I *really* didn't want to get up!

But it was my job. It was time to get to work. I struggled to my feet, stretched, and gave a good shake before I hopped down from the front porch. With a little bit of luck, the Daybreak Patrol would be quick, and I could still squeeze in a quick doggie nap before our people got up.

Our cows were already grazing. There was no smell of coyotes or other dogs. When I checked the barn, Chester, Tabby, and Grace were on duty, keeping the rats and mice away from the cow feed. Our three barn cats weren't all that sociable. They weren't friends—not even with our people. They did their job, though, so Rex and I left them alone.

Daybreak was calm and quiet, so, wagging my tail, I trotted back to the porch for my little doggie nap. I'd just rested my chin on my paws when I heard the door open. It was Ann. She slipped through the opening, as quiet as she could, and very softly shut the door behind her.

So much for my doggie nap!

I felt a little shiver race up the fur on my back when I saw what she was carrying in her hand.

"This is totally disgusting!" I yelped. "I can't stand it!"

"Knock it off," Rex growled.

The sound came from deep in his throat, a tone so low that my Ann—most people animals, for that matter—could never hear it. "Quit being such a wimp," he continued. "Take it like a dog."

Ann latched onto my neck. Then she shoved something over my snout. For a moment or two, I couldn't even see. It smelled of cloth and of the big rubber doll that Nicole used to play with. Ann pushed it farther. Now I could see. Only the cloth smushed one of my ears flat. The strap under my neck was way too tight. I could still breathe, and it didn't hurt—but it was downright uncomfortable.

I flopped my head back and forth, trying to at least get my ear back. It didn't work. Instead, the cloth slipped so I could only see out of one eye. While I was shaking and wiggling my head, I felt Ann place something on my back. I turned to see out of the eye that wasn't covered. It was one of the cloths that Chrissy wrapped around herself when she cooked sausage for breakfast.

When Ann started tugging on the two straps on the cloth, I knew what was coming next. I took a deep breath and held it.

Sure enough, she wrapped the straps around my tummy a couple of times, then pulled them tight as she could. She didn't know how to keep the straps together like Chrissy did. I held my breath so long that my eyes crossed. When she turned to pick up something else, I let the air out. Quickly, I sucked in another breath, but not too much. That way, the cloth straps hung loose enough for me to breathe, but not so loose that Ann would pull them again.

I glanced toward the sound of Rex's tail thumping at the far end of the porch. When he saw me watching, his left ear, right eyebrow, and left whiskers said, "If you try to shake the hat and dress off now, she'll just put them back on. Hang in there. Chrissy should be up anytime now to fix

3

breakfast. She'll see Ann isn't in her room and come to find her."

"Right," I snorted.

Ann stepped back to look at me. It was hard, but I stood still and let her admire her work. She smiled, then frowned, and finally adjusted the bonnet that smelled of Nicole's doll. She shoved and wiggled it until I could see out of both eyes. But when she did, it crunched both my ears down. I shot Rex a disgusted look.

All of a sudden, Ann wrapped an arm around my neck. With her free hand, she reached into the pocket of her pajamas.

Rex's tail stopped in mid-wag. His eyes got big.

"What?" I pleaded with my eyebrows. "What's she doing?"

Rex didn't answer. He just lowered his head and buried his snout between his paws.

Ann had a small plastic tube in her hand. She tugged at it until it came apart, and then she began twisting it until a chunk of red stuff appeared from one end. Tightening her armlock around my neck, she pushed the nasty-looking, foul-tasting, yucky red stuff against my mouth, teeth, and—

"Ann?" Kevin scolded. "You *know* you're not supposed to go outside without telling your mom or me. And that's Nicole's bonnet. You're not supposed to bother her things. What are you doing to that poor dog?"

The second Ann let go, I sprang to my feet. The cloth around my middle fell off, but I had to use my front paws two or three times before I could scrape the bonnet off my head.

"Ann's almost twenty-eight marks old," I whined once I felt Rex and I were far enough from the house to be safe. "She's old enough that she shouldn't be doing stuff like this."

Rex followed me to the far side of Chrissy's garden. He was only a few feet away, but I didn't know whether he could understand me or not. That's because I was still trying to lick the foul red stuff off my mouth and front teeth.

I guess he did understand, because he moved right in front of me and touched his nose to mine.

"You know people animals don't grow as fast as we do. Their marks are different than ours."

"What do you mean, different?"

"Every two moons is a mark of our life," Rex explained. "We add another half for a very cold winter or if we have a really hot summer. But people are slow to mark. My Nicole couldn't even walk until she was twenty-one marks old. Your Ann started walking when she was eighteen marks. In our marks, Ann would be nearly twenty-eight, but in people marks, she is not even five yet. Give her some time."

I licked my lips again, scraped my tongue against the roof of my mouth, and rubbed the

5

other side of my head on the grass. "But dogs aren't supposed to wear dresses and bonnets—especially boy dogs."

"Quit your griping. It's just lipstick." Rex tilted his head to the side. "I think that's what Chrissy called it. You think that stuff is nasty—one time, when Nicole was about Ann's age, she got some stuff called perfume from Chrissy's room. You talk about nasty! It was worse than gettin' sprayed by a skunk. I rolled in everything I could find—cow patties, dirt, even a dead rat I found in the field. I spent half a day standing in the creek to see if the water would take the stink away. Lipstick is nothing."

Rex always thought his stories were better than mine. Every time I had something bad to tell him, he had a story that was even worse.

"But it's just not fair to treat me like that," I mumbled finally.

"Enough griping about how mistreated you are. Looks like we got work to do."

I turned to see where the old dog's nose was pointing.

Down the hill and past the house, a big truck was backing up to the metal gate of our cattle pens. Guess I'd been so busy fussing and rubbing the lipstick off, I hadn't even heard the noise from the motor.

"Well," I muttered to myself, "there went my morning nap."

Chapter 2

I shook the dry grass from my face and sides, then raced off to see what was going on.

When I sprinted past the house, I let out my best bark. "There's a truck on our property! Somebody's here. You better come and take a look!"

The cows in the field began moving closer to check out the commotion.

"Who is it?" they all mooed together.

More bellowing came from inside the trailer. "Who's out there? Who mooed that?"

"Are we there, yet?" A little bellow came from inside.

Rex was getting old. Panting and puffing, he finally caught up with me. He sniffed the trailer, then turned to me.

"Only sixteen cows," he said. "It shouldn't take too long. Should be an easy morning."

My cows walked around in circles as they watched the trailer. I kept barking, letting them know I was here, and telling everyone it was all right. My old herd, as well as whoever was in the trailer, needed to know that I was a good guard dog.

A man swung the door open, hung his feet over the running board, and dropped to the ground. He pulled a dusty cap from his head and slapped it against his leg. The face and the familiar smell took the bristle out of my hair.

"Hey, Hoss." The man smiled at me. "How you doin' this morning? Is there anyone home?" The friendly voice made my tail wag. He reached down, patted my head with one hand, and scratched Rex behind the ears with the other. "How are you doing, old Rex? Still chasing those rabbits?" He strolled toward the house. Rex and I followed.

He was lucky that we knew him so well. We kept on barking, just to make sure our family would know that Tony, Chrissy's brother, was here.

We only took a few steps when the door to the house burst open. Nicole and Ann came running out in their pajamas. Kevin and Chrissy followed them.

"Hey, Rex," I asked, making sure I wasn't too

close to Tony's heels. "If Ann is four in people marks, how old is Nicole?"

Rex closed his eyes, thinking. "Nine. Almost ten." He had to stop, really quick, because when he had his eyes closed, Tony stopped to greet Kevin, and Rex almost ran into him.

"Almost ten," I repeated. "Thanks."

"Hoss! Rex! Hush your barking. You know Tony," Kevin scolded.

We got quiet.

"Uncle Tony!" both girls squealed at the same time. "Did you bring us anything?"

The big man swooped Nicole up in one arm and Ann in the other. He swung them around a couple of times, then set them gently on the ground.

With all the excitement, I just couldn't stop myself. I started bouncing around all three of them, yipping and wagging my tail. The girls reached out, hoping Tony would pick them up again.

"Now, girls!" Chrissy said, trying to calm them. "Settle down."

"You made good time with this load, Tony," Kevin said. "We weren't expecting you until late this afternoon."

"Easier to move during the night." Tony ran his fingers through his hair, then put the dusty cap back on his head. "Cows are more settled, and there's not nearly as much traffic on the road."

9

"What did you bring us?" Kevin peered into the open slots at the front of the big trailer. The girls raced over.

"What did you get *us*?" Nicole insisted.

"Hang on, girls. You'll see in a little bit. Kevin, the ones in the back are yours. There are six cows. Nice and healthy. Three of them with calves." He shook his head. "No, two, really. The little bull calf is already weaned, but they sold him and his mother as a pair."

Kevin led the way to the back of the trailer. "Let's get some hay spread out so we don't have to play rodeo with those other cows. Chrissy, get the girls and drop a round bale over there." Kevin pointed to the pasture, away from the gate opening.

"Come on, girls." Chrissy waved. "The boys have work to do, and so do we."

"But what did you get us, Unca Tony?" Little Ann wrapped herself around Tony's leg.

"Go help your mother." Tony smiled. "I'll show you as soon as we get these cows out of the trailer. They've been cooped up a long time. *You* wouldn't want to be stuck all night in a trailer with these old cows, would you? They need to check out their new home." Tony lifted Ann into the air, then handed her to Chrissy.

Holding Ann in one arm, Chrissy wrapped her other around Nicole's shoulder. They walked to the old yellow Ford pickup truck with the hay spear on the back. She opened the door and hoisted Ann in first. Nicole didn't need any help.

Chrissy drove up to a large round bale of prairie hay and turned the truck around. She stopped and brought the hay spear down. We all watched as she backed the truck so that the spear would go right in the middle of the bale. As she moved something inside the cab, the hay slowly lifted off the ground.

Rex and I followed Kevin to open the gate, then helped him shoo our cows away from the opening. Chrissy and the girls drove through. Our cows immediately followed the hay that dangled from the back of the truck.

My tail wagged. With our cows out of the pen, unloading the new ones would be a lot easier. It might turn out to be a pretty good morning after all. Maybe I would have time to take that little doggie nap that Ann interrupted with her "dress the dog" bit.

A loud commotion from inside the trailer chased all thoughts of a nap from my head. There was stomping and banging. The whole trailer jostled up and down.

"You shove me and my mother again, I'm gonna flatten you," someone mooed. "I'll butt you so hard, you'll end up outside this thing. I'll kick you clear through the roof. I'll—"

"Calm down, dear," a mother cow mooed softly. "It's very crowded in here. We can hardly breathe without bumping each other. I'm fine, and so are you."

But whoever was making the commotion just kept at it. Now the trailer was rocking back and forth.

Maybe it wasn't going to be such an easy morning, after all.

Chapter 3

I started for the trailer to see who—or what—was causing all the fuss. Before I got a chance to hop up and put my front paws on one of the rails so I could look inside, Chrissy drove back through the gate and parked beside Tony's truck. I took off as fast as I could.

Sometimes Ann forgot to use the step. I reached them before Chrissy even had time to turn the engine off. As soon as the door opened, I jumped up and put my front paws on the running board. Nicole held the door with one hand and hopped out just fine. Ann *didn't* hold on to the door; and even with me there, reminding her where the step was, she missed that too.

Luckily for her, I was there.

She tumbled out the door, grabbing me

around the head to try and catch herself. I was there to break her fall and give her something soft to land on, but both of us rolled to the ground.

"Get away, Hoss!" Kevin yelled.

"It's okay, Daddy. He didn't hurted me." Ann grabbed my ear to help pull herself up. I yelped.

Tony turned to Kevin. "Everybody's okay," he called. "Ann just missed the step coming out of the truck and landed on Hoss. They're both fine."

Closing the door, Tony walked back to Kevin. "We better get these ladies out of here. I've still got an hour's drive to Hobart with the rest of this load."

He glanced down at Ann. "And . . . somebody needs a present!"

"Where's *my* present?" I yipped. I sat down and raised both front paws.

"Hey, old Hoss. Just 'cause I always bring something for the girls, what makes you think you and Rex are getting a treat?" Tony laughed as he reached down to scratch behind my ears.

"You always bring us a treat, too!" I barked.

"Come on, Hoss. You can help get these cows out and into the corral. I never could figure how a nice German shepherd like you managed to end up doing the work of a Border collie or an Australian shepherd. You should be protecting a bank, not a farm."

"This work is too important for a collie," I answered with a wag of my tail. "Let me at those cows—I'll show 'em who's boss!"

Tony got back in the truck. The cows in the pasture didn't even look up from their hay when he started the noisy engine. He backed up slowly, until Kevin finally whistled. Once the trailer stopped, Kevin turned to Chrissy. "Will you shut that gate to the pasture? I think these new cows will settle down quicker if we leave them in the big pen for a day or two."

Nicole and Ann raced ahead of their mother to the pasture gate. Both girls jumped on and rode it as it swung shut. Chrissy latched the gate, and we all hurried back to the trailer.

Kevin glanced at Nicole and Ann. "Out of the pen, girls." He motioned with his thumb. "We don't know how these cows are going to act."

Tony strolled to the back of the trailer. "Got the right side against the post," he told Kevin. "When I pop the latch, you pull the gate against your side so they can't get through that way."

Kevin nodded his agreement, then quickly glanced to see if the girls were safe.

All three climbed up on the fence so they could watch. Chrissy was sitting on the top rail, with her arm wrapped around Ann. It made my tail wag. Clumsy as that child was, I was glad that Chrissy had a good hold on her. I turned my attention back to the trailer and waited.

"You too, Hoss. You know those cows won't come out with you there." Kevin snapped his fingers, then pointed beside his right boot. "Sit."

Immediately, I darted under the bottom rail of the fence, ran to him, and dropped my rear end to the ground. Ears perked, I waited.

Tony grabbed the latch. Kevin held the gate.

"Everybody ready?" They both called. "Here goes."

Tony pulled. Kevin swung the gate open and held it against the fence post. And . . .

Nothing happened.

Kevin glanced inside. Tony glanced inside.

"Come on, ladies," Kevin called. "Everybody out!"

Still nothing.

Both men slapped a hand against the trailer. They banged it three or four times.

Nothing.

"Guess they need a little encouragement." Tony sighed and strolled to the cab of the truck. From the bed of the pickup, he pulled out a metal bar, then came back and gently shoved it through the slots in the trailer. There was a lot of clunking and shuffling as the cows began to move around, but not a single one of them came out.

I hopped to my feet. "Want me to get 'em out?" I yipped.

Kevin snapped his fingers. Instantly, I plopped back on my rump.

Finally, one cow stepped down. She was black with a trail of white splotches on her back. It was hard to sit still, but I sat and watched. I was ready to work. I just needed to hear the word.

Two black cows followed her. A big red cow with white splotches stepped to the ground. She had a calf that looked just like her. Another red cow, with a white face, came out next. Her calf was all red. Finally, the last cow and calf stood at the end of the trailer.

"What in the world is that?" Kevin asked, stretching up on his tiptoes to look inside.

"Those two are Belted Galloways," Tony announced with a grin. "Don't they look great? Especially the calf?"

"I've never seen cows colored like that." Kevin stretched again and squinted into the opening.

"Think that breed started out in Scotland." Tony rattled the bar against the slots again. "I've seen a few of them since I started hauling cattle."

"Our Oklahoma summers get pretty hot. Can they handle the heat?"

Tony nodded. "Seem to do just fine. That little fella's built pretty good, don't you think? Thick shoulders. Big rump. Good-lookin' little calf." He nudged the cow with the end of the metal bar.

The mother moved cautiously from the protection of the trailer. As soon as her front hooves touched the dirt, she turned to look at her calf. He backed away from the opening.

"Come on, honey," the mother encouraged. "There's no reason to be afraid."

"I'm not scared!" The calf snorted. "I'm brave. I'm not scared of *anything!*"

Only as soon as he snorted, he disappeared back inside the trailer.

Tony shoved the bar through one of the slots in the trailer and clanked it around until it hit the other side.

"We don't belong here!" the calf bellowed from inside. "This isn't the right place!"

"Come on, baby," Tony urged. "Let's go."

Kevin reached an arm inside and popped him on the rump.

Suddenly, the little guy bolted. Tail flying, he shot off the end of the trailer. Hooves barely touched the ground as he raced to the far end of the big lot. And . . .

Crashed smack-dab into the fence.

The little guy must have been more hard-headed than I thought. He simply bounced off and charged in another direction. He hit the fence again, right under where the girls were. Chrissy squealed, grabbed Nicole and Ann, and managed to keep all three of them balanced on the top rail. Then the calf tore off to crash into the fence on the far side of the lot.

"That's it," Kevin growled. "He's either going to break his fool neck or hurt somebody. Hoss!"

I shot under the bottom fence rail and raced across the lot. Barking and snapping at the calf's heels, I turned him away from the fence and headed him toward his mother. *Now, this is the way it's supposed to work,* I thought. *Go hide behind your mom for a while. I'll sit and watch until you calm down. Then we can all have breakfast, and I can get my treat, and . . .*

Only he didn't run behind his mom to hide, the way most calves do. Right before he reached her, he turned to the right and slammed on the brakes. Dust belched from beneath his hooves as he slid to a stop. The reddish-brown cloud rolled and tumbled into the air, so thick that it hid the other cows from my view. Then—in the blink of an eye . . .

He charged.

I spun around, but the little guy came so quick and unexpected, I didn't even have time to dodge. All I could do was run. He was so close, I could feel the dust exploding from beneath those sharp little hooves, just inches from my tail.

This was not *the way it was supposed to work.*

Chapter 4

"First time I've ever seen Hoss get chased clean out of a cattle pen!" Tony was laughing so hard, he could barely stand. He leaned down to pick up his cap.

"First time I ever saw you laugh your hat off," Kevin chuckled.

As far as I was concerned, it wasn't the least bit funny. It was the second time in one day that I'd been embarrassed. The first: getting stuck in a dress and bonnet. Then I got chased out of my own cow lot by some crazy little calf. It was almost more embarrassment than a self-respecting cow dog could stand.

"That doggone calf ain't gonna run me out of my own pen. I'll show him! I'll grab his nose and flip him. I'll show him who's boss! I'll even rip that nose clean off of him, if I have to. I'll—"

"Oh, knock it off," Rex interrupted with a growl. "The little guy's just scared. Give him some time to settle down."

Ignoring him, I circled around in front of the truck and trailer so I could come out on the side away from Chrissy and the girls. I was panting so hard, my tongue almost dragged the ground.

Rex didn't follow me. His tail didn't even twitch. He simply sat and watched.

By the time I got to the fence, I'd had a chance to catch my breath. The little calf was still trying to figure out where I had gone. Slick as could be, I slipped under the fence, raced up behind him, leaped, and nipped him right on the rump.

"Ouch!" His moo sounded more like a squeak. Then he kicked. The hoof missed me—I was moving too fast. I raced about ten yards in front of him, turned, and snarled.

"That hurt," he complained.

"It didn't hurt. I just nipped you. I could have brought you to your knees."

"How?"

"All I have to do is—" I caught myself just in time. "None of your business. But I could. Now, quit all this foolishness. Go stand by your mother and stop running."

"I don't take orders from you. You're just an old dog!" The calf glared at me. Dust clouds flew as he pawed the ground with his front hoof.

"What do you mean, you don't take orders from me?" I felt the hair bristle to a ridge down my back. "I'm the farm dog. I'm doing my job."

He charged again. This time I waited till the last second. Then I jumped, tucked my tail, and darted from his path. He slid to a stop. Shaking his head and throwing slobbers all over the place, he looked around to see where I had gone. I watched for another charge. Sure enough, here he came. Dodging and darting clear across the lot, I managed to slip in behind him before we reached the far side. Once there, I sprinted up beside him to keep him from slamming into the fence. Then I edged closer and kept turning him so he wouldn't hurt himself.

The calf ran and kicked. I chased and dodged. Dirt and dust flew into my face as the little guy skidded one way, then the other. Zigging and zagging, darting and dodging, I finally managed to herd him back toward the other cows.

"Get over here!" Mother Cow scolded with a stomp of her hoof. "As soon as *you* stop running, *he'll* quit bothering you."

"Leave me alone, dog!"

All the new cows stood in a row, just staring at us as we made two more laps around the big corral.

My eyes were on him, but with all the dust, sometimes it was kind of hard to see. I blinked, trying to get the gritty feel to go away. My nose started twitching and itching. I knew what was coming next. This was bad. I was in big trouble, if I had to . . . had to . . .

Oh, no. Here it comes!

"Achoo! Achoo!" The sneezes stopped me in my tracks. "Achoo! Achoo! Achoo!"

When I quit sneezing, I shook my head and opened my eyes to see where the calf was. I expected him to charge—to be so close, I had no chance of escape. He was *standing* right in front of me. His face was only inches away from mine.

"*Gesundheit*," he said.

"Huh?" I perked my ears. "What did you just say?"

"*Gesundheit*. It means good health," the calf answered.

"*I* know what it means," I fibbed. "How do *you* know what it means?"

Behind me I could hear Ann. "Mama, look at Hoss and Cookie!"

I turned an ear in their direction but kept my eyes on the little calf. Tired eyes looked back at me.

"My last home was with Mr. and Mrs. Nightingale," the calf explained. "Every time Mrs. Nightingale came to the barn, she would sneeze. Sometimes she'd sneeze and sneeze and sneeze, just like you did. And every time Mr. Nightingale would say, '*Gesundheit.* Blessings to you, dear wife.'"

"Look, Uncle Tony. Hoss and Cookie are talking," Ann cried. "Look. Look at them!"

"Who's Cookie?" Tony asked.

"The little calf. He looks like a cookie. You know—he's black on the front, white in the middle, and then black on his hind end. Like a cookie."

"Like an Oreo cookie, Uncle Tony," Nicole explained.

"Hoss and Cookie are talking to each other," Ann repeated.

I glanced over at the fence. Tony was holding Ann on the wooden rail. Nicole stood on the second plank, looking into the corral at us. Kevin and Chrissy watched, too.

"They *do* look like they're talking to each other," Chrissy said, rubbing the back of Kevin's neck. "Don't you think?"

"I think Hoss is staring him down. Showing him who's boss."

"But see how they're looking at each other. See how they're wiggling their ears and turning their heads from side to side. It's almost like they're having a conversation."

"Chrissy, I expect the girls to say silly stuff like that. But you're their mother. You know animals can't talk to each other." Kevin shook his head and kind of rolled his eyes at her. "You sure you been getting enough sleep?"

"Daddy," Ann interrupted, reaching over and tugging at Kevin's shirtsleeve. "Can we call him Cookie?" When Kevin lifted her in his arms, she grabbed him around the neck. "Please, Daddy? Please. Please! Pretty please?"

"I think Cookie is the perfect name," Chrissy agreed. She turned to Nicole. "What do you think, honey?"

Nicole grabbed her mother's hand and squeezed. "Can we name all of them?"

"Maybe. But not right now. We need to leave these cows alone to let them get used to their new home."

"Your mom's right," Kevin said, turning toward the house.

The calf kept staring at me. I guess he was expecting another sneeze. Then I noticed Tony staring at the calf. "How's your bull doing, Kevin?"

Kevin shrugged. "Old Benji bull is due for some pasture time. He may have a year or so left in him, but I definitely need to start looking. Why?"

Tony kept staring at the calf. "Oh, no reason."

Kevin pushed his hair back before he put his hat on. "I'll look the calves over when we work them in October. Probably end up buying another Angus from the Lamar Ranch."

"I like the looks of that Belted Galloway. Cookie . . . the girls sure picked up on that Oreo thing. I didn't even see it." Tony stepped to the bottom board of the wooden fence as he stared at the calf. "Good-looking little guy."

Kevin nodded his agreement. "He's built good." Then he gave a little chuckle. "But the last thing we need around here is a wild, crazy bull."

"You boys coming?" Chrissy called as she headed for the house. "Might be able to rustle up a little breakfast. I'll even start a fresh pot of coffee."

"Be right there, sis." Tony hopped off the fence, jammed his cap back on his head, and took one last glance toward the pen. "Good-looking calf, Kevin," he repeated. "Maybe he'll calm down—make you a right good bull."

Once everyone had gone, the calf gave a little snort. "So what are we going to do?"

"What do you mean?" I wiggled my whiskers.

"Are you going to chase me again?"

"Hoss," Kevin called over his shoulder. "Come on, boy!"

I didn't take my eyes off the crazy calf. "If you want me to chase you, I will. But I'd rather go with my family. Tell you what—you stop being a total idiot and I'll quit chasing you."

"I am *not* a total idiot. I'm a Belted Galloway." He stood up real straight and puffed out his chest.

"Whatever." I shrugged my ears, turned, and trotted off.

Chapter 5

Beside me, Rex was already chomping his breakfast. I stood over my food dish and whined. Chrissy reached down and rubbed my face before she poured the chunks of dry food into my bowl.

"Hey, girls! Come look what I have for you." Tony pulled two sacks out of his jacket. He held them behind his back. "Nicole, left hand or right?"

Nicole stood in front of Uncle Tony and stared from one shoulder to the other.

"Hurry, Nicole. I want to pick." Ann stepped around her sister.

Nicole took a step back. "It's okay, Ann. You choose first."

"Are you sure, big sister?" Tony teased. "I always had to wait for your mom, because she was older."

"It's okay. I know whatever you brought us I'll be happy!"

"Okay. Pick a hand, Ann. Left?" Tony leaned one shoulder forward. "Or right?" He leaned the other.

"I want that one!" Ann pointed to Tony's left shoulder.

"Close your eyes first. You, too, Nicole." Tony brought his arms from behind his back. He held one sack in front of Ann and the other in front of Nicole. "Okay, open!"

The girls' eyes flashed wide. They each grabbed a sack and started digging inside.

"How cute!" Nicole exclaimed, as she pulled out a red and white stuffed cow.

"Thank you, Uncle Tony!"

"Mine looks like Cookie!" Ann giggled. "Well, almost like Cookie."

"Daddy, Mommy, look! Uncle Tony got us our very own cows." Nicole held up hers. Long floppy legs dangled from her hand. "Mine looks like the red calf, and Ann's is black and white, like Cookie."

"Let me see." Chrissy reached for the toy in Nicole's hand. "These are really cute, Tony. Where did you get them?"

"I found them at a western store in Tulsa. I didn't know you were going to end up with matching calves." Tony scratched his head.

"Do you have time for breakfast?" Chrissy reached for the soap.

"Sure. I'd like to get the rest of the load to Hobart before ten, but I think I can squeeze in a few minutes to eat." Tony poured himself a cup of coffee before he plopped in the chair close to me. Leaning over, he reached down to rub my back as he sipped his coffee.

After breakfast I curled up on the floor near the back door. Rex came to lie beside me. I sort of expected him to tease me about getting chased out of the pen. Either that or tell me what *he* would have done with the little calf. But he simply curled up next to me and closed his eyes. Seemed like a good idea to me. As soon as I had a little nap, I'd go check on the corral and find out more about my new cows. Especially that darn little cookie-colored calf.

I'd just drifted off when my keen ears heard a commotion. I stood up and shook. Pushing the screen door open with my nose, I saw movement down in the lot. *Here we go again,* I sighed, and trotted off to see what was wrong.

"All right, ladies. What's going on?"

Low, angry moos came from my mother cows.

"What's wrong?" I urged.

"It's that *bossy* calf," Sissy bawled. "He's going to be nothing but trouble. You'd better get control of him . . . and soon."

Several low moos followed in agreement.

The little Belted Galloway shoved his way to the fence. "That big mean red cow was ordering my mom around. My mom does *not* take orders from her."

I glanced at Jewel. "What was he doing?"

"Sissy's still trying to be boss—trying to get her bluff in on his mom. The little guy got upset. Nothing, really. I figure he just needs some time, that's all."

"Sorry about that," said the calf's mother as she squirmed her way to the fence. "He's always tried to protect me, whether I need protecting or not. It's his age. He's no longer a baby, but he's not grown up yet, either. Still . . . well, he thinks he's ready to be the herd bull. I hope he'll adjust quickly."

"Do you have any control over him?" I asked.

"You may ask *me* any question you might have about *me!*" The calf butted his way between his mom and the fence. "*And,* for your information, her name is Victoria."

"Not much," the mother cow admitted, trying to ignore his interruption. "He just needs some time. This is his first big move."

"Well, for now, Victoria, can you try to keep things down a bit?" I stared at the calf. "This place has been running just fine. I know that you need some adjustment time, but I think we can do it peacefully."

"We'll work on it—won't we, son?" The mother cow nuzzled the calf's neck.

Lowering his head, the little calf kicked dirt, then charged toward me. His attack took me by surprise. I jumped back, and nearly toppled over.

I got my feet under me just as the calf bumped into the board fence. He hit it so hard, it made the metal gate rattle.

"Leave us alone, you nasty old dog! I'll take care of my herd." Eyes tight, he shook his head from side to side. Slobbers drizzled onto the fence.

I glared at the little calf. "This isn't over, kid."

All my people were outside when I got back to the house. Tony was hugging the girls. Nicole had her stuffed cow draped over her arm, and Ann was clutching hers against her chest. I whiffed the air. Everything seemed to be in order—no strangers or bad animals around the house. Perking my ears, I listened for coyotes. Nobody was talking. Everything was fine, so I led the way to Tony's truck.

"Hey, Hoss. Did you think I forgot you?" Tony pulled three dog biscuits out of his pocket and laid them in a row on his hand.

Tail wagging, I took the first one. Gulped it down. The second one went pretty quick, too.

"Are you ready, big Hoss?" Tony balanced the last one on my nose. I sat motionless, waiting for the command.

"Go, Hoss!" Tony said. With a quick jerk of my head, I flipped the biscuit off my nose and grabbed it with my teeth.

"Good boy!"

Tony's pat and praise made my tail wag. He kissed Nicole and Ann on the cheek, then gave Chrissy a big hug before he hopped into his truck.

I stood watching with my family as Tony revved the engine. As soon as he headed down our road, I walked my family to the house, then trotted to my lookout spot.

A ridge of dirt (Kevin and Chrissy called it a terrace) ran between the house and the corral. The highest spot on it was about a hundred dog-trot paces southwest of the back door. From there I couldn't see Rex, but I knew he would be guarding Chrissy's flower garden at this time of day. I could see just about everything else on the farm: the barn, the corral, most of the pasture where my cows usually grazed, the back door of our house, and the driveway. It was the best place on the whole farm to keep an eye on things. Life was good.

Tony's truck and trailer kicked up dust on the gravel road. After he topped the hill and was out of sight, the dust finally drifted off with the breeze. I turned my attention back to the corral.

My cows stood near the wooden fence. Old Sissy had her head pressed against one of the boards. The new big red cow—the one with the calf—had her head pressed against the board from the other side. They both seemed to be pushing really hard.

I sprang to my feet and headed that direction.

Sissy was our number two Mama. Even though she was second in command—right under Jewel, our main Mama—Sissy still tried to boss the other cows around. Looked to me like she was already starting in on one of the new ladies.

They were both so busy pushing at each other, neither of them noticed me until I was standing under the corral fence, almost between them.

"All right," I snarled, showing my teeth. "What's going on now?"

Startled, both jumped back. Sissy wobbled her head and looked down at me. "Oh, nothing," she lied. "We were just getting acquainted."

The red cow didn't say anything.

"That's fine," I said, with a shrug of my ears. "Just don't get too 'acquainted.'" I stretched up and sniffed the wood they'd been pushing on. "You break part of Kevin and Chrissy's fence, and it will make me *very* unhappy."

Sissy swished at a fly with her tail, then strolled off.

"You ladies doing all right in here?" I asked.

"We're fine," one of the black cows mooed. "The hay is very good."

"Got plenty of fresh water in the trough?" I

bent down to squeeze under the fence so I could check it myself.

"Get back!" the little cookie-colored calf snorted. He pawed the dirt with a front hoof. "Don't come in my pen."

"Excuse me?" I felt my ears twitch, then perk straight up. "*Your* pen?"

"You come in here, I'll butt you! I'll run you down this time. I mean it!"

"Hey, kid. Chill. I'm just checking things out. Making sure everyone is okay and feels welcome. What's your problem?"

The calf snorted and pawed the dirt with his other hoof. "This is my home now. *I'll* take care of *my* herd. It's my right."

"I think you're a little confused, kid." I kicked the dirt with one hind foot, then the other. "You live here . . . but this is *my* farm and *I'm* in charge."

The calf tossed his head and let out a little snort. "I don't think you understand, sir. Either that or you're not listening. I, sir, am *royalty!*"

"Royalty?" One ear arched, the other drooped. "What's that?"

The little calf shook his head and shot me a look as if I were the dumbest dog he'd ever met.

"My ancestors came from Galloway in Scotland. My great-great-great-great-grandfather, Sir Winston Berkshire Galloway, was the sire for an entire new breed: the Belted Galloway. My great-great-grandfather was Reserve World Champion in the prestigious annual stock show at Wiltstershire, England. My grandfather was the first Belted Galloway to ever leave our homeland and come to the New World. And my father was Reserve Grand Champion at the Pennsylvania state fair three years ago. My mother and I have 'papers.' We can trace our heritage back to the beginning of our breed. We are champions. We are royalty!"

He raised his nose so high in the air that if it had been raining, the poor little thing would have drowned.

"Look, kid. You're a *calf.* I'm the farm dog. I'm in charge of *everything* here on the farm, and that includes *you!*"

He lowered his head and pawed the dirt.

I spun around and kicked at the dirt with my hind feet. Using both of them, and kicking as fast as I could, I thrashed up a cloud of dust so thick that the poor little guy disappeared. When the dust cleared, I was halfway back to the house, and he was coughing and snorting, trying to get the dust out of his snout.

Doggone calf, I thought with a wag. *Serves him right.*

Chapter 6

With the new cows in the separate pen, I had a few days to study them before my real work started. I had to figure out if any of them would be a problem. Well, any others besides the calf Nicole and Ann called Cookie. I spent a lot of time just watching.

The first day was uneventful. Rex watched for rabbits, I stayed at my lookout place. The new cows munched on hay and explored their small space. My old cows stayed away from the new ones. They acted like nothing was different. It was a restful day.

The next morning, my ladies started talking to the new cows. There was a lot of bawling, but there wasn't much activity going on. I still had time to rest my eyes. I was just getting comfortable when I heard someone calling.

"Hoss. Come here, Hoss!" The sound of Ann's voice was close. I jumped up and searched the yard near the house. She wasn't there.

"Over here," I barked to her.

"There you are, Hoss. Good puppy." Ann raced to the top of the terrace, where I stood watch. Just as she got to me, she stumbled, reached out, and grabbed a handful of hair. I winced, but it didn't hurt enough to make me yelp. Ann smiled down at me and patted my head. "Come on, let's go see Cookie."

I perked my ears and listened for Chrissy or Nicole. Then I stretched my neck and looked for Kevin. Nobody!

"Come on, Hoss." Ann pulled my ear. "Let's find Cookie."

I dug my paws into the ground. Ann could get stepped on. She was too little to be playing near our cows. Especially the new ones—and Cookie, in particular. He needed more time to learn the rules of the farm.

"Come on, puppy. Let's go." Ann's little arms stretched around my neck. I stood still. Then suddenly, I shoved against her so she would go the other way. When she let go, she lost her balance and fell. Once she got up, she should have headed back toward the house. But instead, she took off running toward the corral.

I'd spent my whole life herding cows. That was easy. All you have to do is bark and get them moving. Then you run around from one side to the other, and keep them headed the way they're supposed to go. If they veer off, you just dart in front of them and get them turned back on course. No problem.

A kid is something else!

Just when you think you have them on the right track, they pull your ear or grab you by the tail.

I bounded around Ann, leaping and jumping in front of her. Bending way down, I dropped my front end on the ground, until my chest was touching the dirt. With my rear in the air, I growled a warning. She just fell down on me and giggled.

"Let's go, Hoss. What's the matter with you? I want to see Cookie."

"You're too little," I growled.

Carefully, I grabbed the seat of her pants. She stumbled and landed flat on her bottom.

"Hoss! You're not supposed to bite me. I'm going to tell Mama!" Ann turned around and headed for the house.

"Hey! I didn't bite you!" I yelped as she stomped off to tattle.

She wasn't even inside yet when I heard a commotion in the field. *Now what?*

Right in the middle of the pasture, Sissy and old Jewel were bellowing at each other. Their horns were only inches apart. I ran between them, barking and snarling. Whatever the argument had been about, it stopped. They both looked at me. With one last glare at Sissy, Jewel stomped her foot and walked away.

I went back to my lookout and checked all of our property before I plopped down in the soft grass. At last, things were calm and quiet. But just as my eyelids were feeling heavy, a movement caught my eye.

Ann! She *wasn't* going back to the house, she was waddling down the hillside. She was heading toward the creek.

I leaped to my feet and charged down the hill. Using my biggest barking voice, I yelped, "Chrissy! Kevin! Somebody! Anybody!"

I couldn't wait for them. I had to stop Ann.

By the time I got to the creek, I was nearly barked out. Ann was stomping in the mud. Her feet and sandals were coated in muck. The water was barely running in the creek, but I guess the mud was just too inviting.

I started barking again. "Chrissy! Come help me with this kid!"

"Hoss. Good dog. You came with me." Ann turned around and reached for me—only her feet were stuck in the mud. She swayed back and forth a couple of times, then plopped down on her rear.

Muddy fingers grabbed at my fur. Ann pulled

herself up, but as soon as she let go, she fell back with a splat.

"Hoss," she whined, "I can't get out."

There were lots of places along the creek that had mud. Some were squishy, others not so bad. Sometimes the cows would get stuck. Their feet would mire down and Kevin would have to get someone to help him get them out. Other times, they were stuck so bad that they would have to get the tractor to help.

Ann had found a squishy place. If she was really stuck as bad as I thought, and I left her . . . well, she could be in trouble—big-time!

On the other hand, she wasn't going any-place. Maybe I could get help.

But what if I couldn't? What if no one came?

Cows are easy. Kids—oh, my gosh!

Chapter 7

I eased my way to the edge of the mud where my feet were still on firm ground. Slowly, I leaned toward Ann. Maybe if she got a hold around my neck and . . .

I yelped. Ann *didn't* grab my neck. Instead, she latched onto both ears. I ducked and jerked free. Shaking my head a few times, I tried to chase the pain away so I could think what to try next.

This time I turned my right side toward her. Slow and easy, trying to keep my left paws on solid ground, I edged closer. It would hurt, but if she could get a good hold on my hair . . . well, it could stand the pain a lot better than my ears. If I jerked, she'd lose her grip, but if I pulled—calm and steady—I just might be able to drag her out.

Ann got a double fistful of hair. I winced, but I

didn't try to run. I leaned my weight to the left. Tried to keep my movements easy, so I wouldn't lose her. Then . . .

My paws started to slip!

I went down on my right side. Ann tried to climb over me. When she did, most of her weight was on my neck and head. If she pushed me down any farther, I'd go under. I had to get up! I had to get away!

Jerking and struggling, I finally managed to escape to solid ground. Ann hung on, but not for long. At least my clambering moved her closer to the edge of the mud, and on her feet.

I tilted my head from one side to the other, studying the situation. Ann was standing up, but still stuck in the mud. Most of my coat was covered with the slimy stuff. If I got close enough for her to get another hold, her little hands would simply slip off.

I didn't know what to do.

It was a hard decision, but finally I gave Ann a quick kiss with a lick of my tongue and raced for the house. I must have been running faster than I thought, because about halfway there I dodged around a big cottonwood tree, and . . .

I slammed smack-dab into Rex. I tried to stop the instant I saw him, only I couldn't. He yelped because it hurt. I yelped because it startled me.

"What's wrong?" He asked after both of us got our senses back. "What's the rush?"

"It's Ann! She's stuck in the mud! I was going for help, and . . ."

"You left her there?" Rex growled. "You don't *ever* leave your girl! Not when she needs help or is in trouble. Not ever!" He growled again—even showed his teeth as he scolded me.

"But I can't get her out. I need help!"

Rex glanced down at the mud on my legs, paws, and all over my right side where Ann had pulled me over trying to get out.

"*I'll* go get help!" He snapped at me. "*You* go back. Stay with Ann. *Now!*"

When I reached the creek, I stopped. On trembling legs, I looked one way, then the other. I felt the hair ridge down my back.

Ann wasn't there!

Far behind me, I could hear Rex barking. I scanned the creek. Maybe she had finally managed to pull her feet from the sloppy, gooey mess and had taken off to explore somewhere else. Or . . . or maybe she was still there, mired so deep in the mud that I couldn't see her. I charged to the spot.

I sniffed. Then my tail wagged—but for only a second. Ann was gone, but her trail was still warm.

I followed it. Squinting, I caught a movement out of the corner of my eye. Covered in mud, Ann was sloshing up the hill toward the rock play-house. A quick glance over my shoulder told me

Rex was following. Chrissy was not far behind him. Wagging my tail and pointing my nose straight toward Ann, I barked, "Here she is!"

"Go, Hoss. Stop her!"

The way Chrissy's voice trembled made the hair ridge up on my back once more. Barking as loud as I could, I raced after Ann.

"Ann! Stop!" I barked.

The playhouse really wasn't a playhouse. It was a huge flat rock that jutted out over a deep crevice. A long time ago, Kevin's aunts and uncles stacked rocks all the way around it, so it looked like what they called a "fort" or a "castle"— whatever that was. When Kevin was little, he and his brother used to play there. Sometimes Chrissy and Kevin took the girls there for picnics.

Trouble was, Ann was way too little to be there by herself. If she wasn't paying attention, or if she climbed on part of the rock wall where the boulders were loose, she could fall. The crevice beneath the edge wasn't very big. But it *was* deep. It was a long ways down, especially for someone as little as my Ann.

Stumbling and clambering my way up the rocks, I finally reached the playhouse. I darted between Ann and the edge of the cliff, but she just ignored me and tried to go around. I barked as loud as I could. She stepped in the other direction. I cut her off, curled my lips—showing my sharp teeth—and snarled at her.

Looking confused, Ann curled her lips back. Then she frowned and tilted her head to one side before shoving her way past me. She took another step toward the edge of the flat rock. There was nothing else I could do. Careful not to grab hold of any skin, I reached up and clamped my teeth on the seat of her pants. Ann tried to keep walking, then struggled a moment. When she realized she wasn't going anyplace, she turned to glare at me.

"Bad dog! You didn't help me get out of the mud," Ann scolded. "Let go."

"Stop right there, young lady," Chrissy called from behind us. Rex scooted out of her way as she raced toward her daughter.

"I want to look over the side!" Ann's feet kept churning.

Chrissy took a deep breath. "One . . . two . . ."

Before Chrissy got to "three," Ann froze in her tracks. Only when she stopped I was still tugging. Little feet shuffled as she tried to keep her balance. Before I could let go, she toppled backward. She landed right on top of me, pinning my head and snout to the hard rock.

Chrissy scurried to us and swooped Ann up in her arms. She hugged her close.

"Young lady! What in the world were you doing?"

"I just wanted to play!" Ann's lip quivered.

"You know you aren't to leave the house without permission. You were supposed to be taking a nap with the rest of us . . . not running around outdoors." Chrissy sat down on the rock with Ann on her lap.

"Hoss was with me." Ann reached up and touched her mother's chin.

"I can see that." Chrissy frowned. "He's covered with mud, just like you are."

I sat next to Chrissy, dropping my chin on her shoulder. Chrissy reached over and rubbed my face. Then she turned back to Ann.

"Don't do that again, young lady. It looks like Hoss worked hard to keep you safe. Rex came to tell me something was wrong. As for you—you *know* you need someone with you. There are too many things that can happen. We have to know where you are. Do you understand?" Cupping Ann's chin in her hand, Chrissy turned her head so her daughter had to look straight in her eyes. "Do you understand?"

"Yes, Mama. I'll stay with Hoss."

"Ann! You have to stay with a *grown-up*. Nicole and Rex and Hoss are fine to play with in the yard. When you leave the yard, an adult has to be with you. Understand?" Chrissy wrapped her arms around Ann.

"Grown-up." Ann sniffed. "Okay."

I felt my ears perk as a sound came to them. When I looked toward the creek, I saw Kevin making his way up the hill. "What are you doing up there?" He called.

"We're just looking things over," Chrissy shouted as she stood up.

Kevin waved for her to come. "Nicole and I are hungry. We're ready to eat."

"We're on our way." Chrissy rubbed behind my ears, then switched Ann to her other arm. "Let's go, kids."

Later that evening, dust flew as my family drove down the driveway. I stood at attention then trotted to my lookout to wait.

When they got back, Kevin was carrying two small dishes of ice cream.

"Here, Hoss. Here, Rex. This is melting fast." He set the bowls down.

"You're good dogs. You both sure helped with Ann this morning." He gently rubbed my ears, then patted Rex on the back.

I checked out the cool stuff in the bowl.

"Pretty tasty!" I said with a wag of my tail.

"Hoss, get a good night's rest. Tomorrow we're going to put all the cows together. I think they're ready. They seem to be pretty calm—all except that little Belted Galloway. He's quite a character." Kevin pulled his cap off, brushed his hair back, then carefully put his cap on once more.

As soon as we finished the ice cream, we moved closer so that my head was under Kevin's left hand and Rex's was under his right. He started rubbing our heads and ears—just the way we had trained him to.

Chapter 8

My plan was to sleep in, but those pesky coyotes started howling before sunup. I stretched before I stepped off the porch. Their yipping and yapping seemed to be about nothing. I strolled away from the house so I wouldn't wake my people and wailed back at them for a few minutes.

Awake now, I decided to see what old Rex was up to before my big day started. He wasn't on the porch, so he was probably out by Chrissy's flowers. I started in that direction, but a scratching sound caught my attention. I followed the sound to Kevin's tractor. I leaned forward to look around one of the huge tires. Three armadillos were digging little holes in the ground. Their snouts were sniffing for grubs, and their dark beady eyes were watching for any bug that might make a tasty meal.

"What are you guys doing?" I growled.

Three heads turned slowly toward me.

"Hey!" I growled again.

"Grubs. We're eating grubs," the smallest one said.

"Well, go eat grubs somewhere else. Kevin doesn't want little holes all over our property."

"Okay. No problem. We're out of here." The armadillos lumbered off across the pasture. Their armored backs rolled, catching the sunlight as they went. I kept my eye on them until they disappeared behind the far terrace.

I found Rex sniffing around some brush near the house.

"Hey, Rex. What are you doing this morning?"

"Stinking rabbits," he grumped. "I spend all spring trying to keep them out of the green beans. Now they're into Chrissy's flower beds. When I chase one of them off, another two sneak in from the other direction. And if I chase *them* away, three more show up while I'm gone. Pesky vermin." He kicked grass with his hind paws.

"Maybe I can help you out tonight."

Rex wagged his tail. "I'd really appreciate that. Having two of us on guard might discourage them. Anything I can do to help *you* today?"

"We're moving the new cows into the pasture this morning. If it works like usual, Kevin will want to separate the calves so we can move them to the other farm."

"You think you can handle it?" Rex asked.

Rex was part hound of some sort, probably basset hound. When he was sad or unhappy, his floppy ears really drooped and his jowls sagged. Before I came to live with our family, Rex had my job. One day, when I was still a pup, Jewel kicked him. He had to go to a place called "the Vet." He could still run and get around, but when it came to working in tight quarters, like the corral . . . well, he just wasn't that quick.

"It's an easy job," I said, nudging his ear with my nose and wagging my tail. "I'll give a howl if I need help, though. Okay?"

Rex's ears bounced when he nodded his head. "Think I'll go to the porch. A little shut-eye ought to help me get ready for an all-nighter with those rabbits. Howl if you need me."

"Thanks, Rex. Soon as I check on the cows, I might come and join you."

He headed for the house, and I went to find my herd. Following the fence line, I made my way to the back pasture. Clouds covered the horizon. The sun was just peeking through when I saw them. I sat down to watch.

Jewel, our lead cow, was grazing near the fence. She was the sweetest, calmest, and gentlest of our ladies. I couldn't imagine her ever kicking at anyone. Even when it came to keeping the other cows in line, she hardly ever butted or kicked.

Jewel kept looking up, checking for any danger and watching the other ladies. Sissy stood near her. Everyone knew that Sissy wanted to be the lead cow. Helen was the babysitter today. Six little calves were nestled in the grass. Even with my sharp eyes, I had to stare hard to count them. Helen stood in the middle, keeping watch. The rest of the herd moved slowly as they grazed on the buffalo grass.

We had some nice cattle. They got along— most of the time. All the ladies were easy to herd. The babies were growing like mad, too. The babysitter cows helped me get them shaped up. They let the calves know that I was in charge, and they followed my orders from the very beginning.

The sun was high overhead when I finally trotted back toward the house. My family should be awake, eating breakfast by now. I took one last look at the herd.

Yep, I thought with wag of my tail, *it's going to be an easy day. Get the babies separated and the new ladies moved quick, and I'll have plenty of time for a nap. Be all rested and ready to help Rex with the rabbits tonight.*

The smell of bacon tugged at my nose long before I reached the steps. It made my mouth water and my tail wag. I scratched on the screen door until Chrissy opened it for me. Kevin sat at the table, holding his coffee cup in two hands. Chrissy went back to her stove. Nicole was shoveling cereal into her mouth, and had her stuffed cow tucked under her arm. Ann was wrapped in her favorite blanket on the couch in the living room.

"Woof," I greeted. Kevin and Chrissy both looked at me.

"Where have you been, old dog?" Kevin rubbed my ears. "Thought we might have to start without you."

"*Grr*. Don't leave me out of this. I can't wait!" I rushed to the back door and bounced up and down with my front paws.

"That's the spirit. You're ready to show 'em, aren't you, Hoss?" Kevin rubbed the spots where my ears connect to my head. I looked up and wagged my tail so hard, my whole rear end swayed back and forth. I wanted to purr, but that was strictly for *loser cats*. When Kevin finally stopped, I nuzzled his hand.

Chrissy put my food bowl beside the stove. Rex was already eating next to the refrigerator. I rushed over to scarf my meal as fast as I could. On "bacon day," both of us usually finished before our family started eating.

It wasn't long before Kevin, Ann, and Chrissy sat down to eat their breakfast. I slipped under the table between Kevin and Ann. Rex sat down on the other side, between Nicole and Chrissy. Ann usually finished off her eggs, then ate her bacon. If I sat quietly under the table by her dangling legs, she would always share her bacon—little pieces, one at a time.

She'd been sharing with me since she was a baby. I'd learned to be discreet while waiting for Ann's treats. Kind of a messy eater, she'd sit in her high chair and drop little tidbits all over the place. When she got bigger, she started dropping stuff into my mouth—on purpose. Rex got the same treats from his Nicole. From watching his technique when I was a pup, I learned that I had to be very gentle or the family would figure out that I was taking snacks from the baby. Kevin fussed at Nicole and Ann, but not too much. That's because he'd slip me a bite or two as well. Chrissy fussed at all of them. But I noticed she'd sneak stuff to Rex when she thought no one was watching. Rex and I *loved* "bacon day." We just tried to keep it a secret, like our Ann and Nicole did.

"We'd better get moving," Kevin announced. "Everybody ready?"

My head clunked the underneath part of the table when I hopped to my feet. I slipped out between the chairs and stood at the door, ready to go. Still chewing the last bit of bacon that Chrissy had slipped him, Rex followed. "You sure you don't need help?"

"Naw. We can handle it."

When everyone but Rex got down to the lot, the new cows seemed to sense that something was going on. The feed Kevin gave them was good, but they were ready for some green grass. All my other ladies had moved closer to the fence in the second pasture, waiting. They must have known something was going to happen, too.

Kevin drove the pickup into the field. The rest of us rode in the back. He stopped the truck, got out, then strolled back to drop the tailgate. I hopped out. Chrissy and Nicole followed. Kevin lifted Ann, put her in the cab of the truck, and shut the door.

"Everybody know what they have to do?" Kevin asked as he shoved his cap down on his head.

"I wait by the gate until you tell me to open it and let the cows out!" Nicole answered.

"And?" Kevin frowned and folded his arms.

"And . . ." Nicole hesitated. "And then I get away from the opening—really fast—and climb up on the fence down by the far corner."

"I close the corner gate," Chrissy said, "as soon as you and Hoss get the calves in."

Kevin smiled. Then tilting his head to the side, he frowned. "Think I'll get the rope out of the truck. We'll tie it to the bottom of the gate. Leave it lying on the ground until we get the calves in, then yank. Kookie as that little Cookie calf is, I don't want you in the pen. Best to work it from the outside."

Chrissy shrugged.

Kevin got the rope from the truck, then looked in the window at Ann. Arms folded, she sat pouting behind the steering wheel. She didn't look at him.

"Ann?"

She still didn't look up.

"*Ann!*"

"I honk the horn if the cows try to get into the feed sacks."

"And?"

She glared out the front windshield.

"And?" Kevin repeated.

"And . . ." She snorted. "*I stay in the truck.*" Without taking a breath, she added, "But why can't I go with Nicole and Mama? I'm a big girl. The new cows won't step on me."

Very gently, Kevin reached into the truck and cupped Ann's chin in his hand. He turned her face so she would look at him, then gave her a kiss right on her little pug nose. "Ann, I know you're a big girl, and I know you can stay out of the way. It's not the new cows I'm worried about. It's our *old* cows that you need to watch. They're used to being fed out of the truck. They love the sweet feed pellets. I think they'll be more interested in meeting the new cows, but if they come to the truck and start getting into the sacks, we're going to have a real mess on our hands. That's why we need you to honk the horn if they get too close. It's an important job. You think you can handle it?"

Ann smiled and nodded her head. But I could smell that she still wasn't happy about being left.

Kevin turned back to Chrissy and Nicole. "Okay. Let's get 'er done."

" 'Gettin' 'er done' " took a lot longer than any of us thought. Kevin ended up climbing the fence three times, Chrissy got rope burns on her hands from that doggone bull calf busting through the half-closed gate, and I had to dart under the bottom rail twice.

"Forget that crazy calf," Kevin finally snarled. "Soon as we get the other two up, we'll let him out with the herd."

Kevin managed to get the two calves into the corner so Chrissy could close the gate. I kept Cookie busy by having him chase me around at the other end of the corral. Kevin never did tell Nicole to open the gate and let the cows out. Instead, he climbed over the fence, put Nicole on the top rail at the far corner, and opened it himself.

The second he stepped aside, Cookie took off like a shot. He ran and bounced, dodging one way, then the other, as if a butterfly, ant, or strange-looking piece of grass had startled him. The rest of the cows trotted through the opening, too. They didn't trot for long. Stopping to munch some of the green grass, they settled and ignored Cookie's antics.

"Go around *outside* the fence," Kevin called to Chrissy. "I don't want you two in the pasture with that crazy idiot running around."

Once Chrissy and Nicole were on their way *and* were on the far side of the barbed-wire fence, Kevin rattled the gate to make sure it was closed. Head down, he kept mumbling stuff to himself about the calf. We had gone only a few steps when Kevin looked up. Suddenly, he stopped. I glanced to see what he was looking at. Then I turned my eyes toward the truck.

Then . . .

My heart stopped. My legs trembled. The hair raised to a ridge down my back, from my ears clear to the tip of my tail.

Ann sat on the open tailgate, with her little legs dangling over the end.

Cookie stood glaring at her, only inches away.

Chapter 9

I charged to protect my girl. I only got to charge about six or seven leaps before Kevin's voice stopped me. His command was sharp and clear, yet barely above a whisper.

"Hoss! Stop!" He snapped his fingers. Pointed to the ground beside his right boot.

I took another step.

Kevin was wrong. The calf was way too close to my Ann. He could butt her and knock her clear off the tailgate. Crazy as he was, he might even jump into the back of the pickup. He might . . .

I took another step.

"Hoss! Here!"

I didn't come "here," but I did sit down. If something happened, I was a few steps closer. A few steps might make all the difference in the world for my Ann.

"Chrissy," Kevin called. His voice was louder than the stern command he had given me. At the same time, his tone was light and almost happy. "Chrissy," he called again. "Stop. Go back on the other side of the fence with Nicole. Don't do anything to startle him."

Chrissy was almost as reluctant as I was. She stopped, but she didn't go back. Even though we were quite a ways apart, I could see her legs shaking—just like mine.

Slow and easy, Kevin took a couple of steps. I moved five more steps closer to Ann.

This time Kevin's whisper was even more gruff than before. "Hoss! Heel!" He snapped his fingers and jabbed it at the ground beside him. "Here! *Right now!*" Reluctant, and glancing over my shoulder at Ann with almost every step I took, I trotted to his side. Moving with my front legs beside his boot, we took three steps. Stopped. Then three more steps.

Ann's little legs swung back and forth as they dangled over the tailgate. They stopped wiggling when she leaned and stretched out her hand to rub Cookie's nose.

"Chrissy? Hoss and I are going to move in real slow. I'll keep talking so the calf knows we're coming. Don't make any quick movements or do anything to startle him. Understand?"

Chrissy nodded.

"Ann, I want you to scoot back. Get away from the tailgate and—"

Kevin didn't finish what he was trying to say. When he looked away from Chrissy and saw what Ann was doing, he knew she wasn't paying a bit of attention to him.

Ann rubbed Cookie's nose with her right hand. With her left hand, she scratched and petted his forehead. She was so close to the end of the tailgate that if she stretched just the tiniest bit more, or if Cookie moved, she'd probably topple off and land right under his hooves.

Kevin started talking again. Not really saying anything, just making his voice sound soft and comfortable. We kept moving, just a few steps at a time. I could see Cookie watching us out of the corner of his eye. He knew we were getting closer but seemed in no hurry to leave Ann.

By the time we were almost to them, the calf's head was practically in her lap. Still watching us, Cookie gently nudged her—sort of scooted her back on the tailgate. Then he raised his head out of her reach and moved to the front of the truck.

As soon as Cookie trotted off to join his mom, Kevin and I raced for Ann. With four legs, instead of just two, I was a lot faster, so of course I beat him. Sliding to a stop in front of the truck, I took up a position between Ann and that doggone little calf. If he doubled back, I'd be there to protect her. Just about the time I got stopped, I heard a noise behind me. It was the sound of Chrissy jumping into the back of the pickup. Even though she had been farther away, she got there just a second or two after I did.

Trembling and shaking, she snuggled Ann close. Then Kevin was there, hugging them both.

Ann was safe. I couldn't understand why Chrissy was crying. Not until Ann asked, "Why are you crying, Mama?"

Chrissy sniffed and wiped her eyes with the sleeve of her blouse. "I'm crying because you scared me, Ann. That's a *big* calf. You're a *little* girl. He could have hurt you. And . . . and I guess I'm crying because . . . because I'm happy you're okay."

"You cry because you're happy?"

Chrissy nodded and sniffed again. "Sometimes."

"I thought I told you to stay in the truck," Kevin's voice was more shaky than mad.

"I *did* stay in the truck."

"I meant in the cab."

"You didn't say in the cab. You said stay in the truck. I never got out once."

Chrissy stopped hugging Ann and held her at arm's length. "Then exactly how *did* you get in the back of the pickup, young lady?"

Ann pointed behind her. "I climbed out the window. Then I hung on, real tight, and put my foot on the back. Then swung around, and . . . *Stayed. In. The. Truck.*"

I glanced over my shoulder. The smug, smart tone of Ann's voice and the look on Kevin's face made my ears flatten and my tail tuck. Sure enough . . .

Ann got the "You could fall and break your neck" speech from Chrissy, followed by the "Cows aren't pets—you could have been trampled" speech from Kevin.

I'd heard them before, when Nicole was about Ann's age. So I turned my attention to the cows.

The "meet 'n' greet" seemed to be going pretty well. There was some bumping and nudging. One of the new cows and one from my herd were doing a bit of light shoving, but it was more like leaning against each other. Mostly, it was simply the ladies' way of saying hello.

I'd just turned to trot back to the pickup when a movement caught my eye. Sissy had her head against the big red cow's side and was shoving as hard as she could. The red cow staggered to keep her balance, but Sissy kept pushing. Finally, the red cow lurched forward, got her balance, and turned on Sissy. Head to head, glaring each other in the eye, they shoved each other back and forth. Then forth and back. Then back and forth again.

It didn't take Sissy long to decide that she was outmatched. But instead of going back to munch grass and mind her own business, she headed toward the mother Belted Galloway. Trouble was, they were way too close to the fence.

Barking and growling, I raced across the pasture and darted between them before they even started.

"You ladies can push and shove all you want," I snarled, showing my sharp teeth. "Just keep it out in the middle of the pasture. We don't need anything knocked down. You tear up Kevin's fence, I'll chase both of you until you can't take another step."

"Excuse me, mutt," Cookie interrupted.

"What now, kid?"

"My cows have the right to figure out their . . . their . . ." He stopped, tilted his head to one side, and looked at his mom. "What did you call it, Mother?"

Victoria stopped glaring at Sissy for just an instant and turned her attention to her son. "Pecking order."

With a snort, Cookie looked back at me and nodded his head. "Yeah. That packing order thing. My cows have the right to—"

"It's *pecking* order," Sissy interrupted.

Cookie's ears tipped forward.

"It means deciding who's in charge, and in

what order," Victoria explained. "Like who is number one cow, who is number two, number three, and so on."

Cookie snorted and stomped his hoof. "Yeah— what she said. My cows have the right to figure that out. They do *not* need any help from a pesky farm dog."

Okay, I thought. *I've tried chasing him. I've tried talking to him, reasoning with him. Nothing seems to work . . . But he didn't hurt Ann, so I owe him one for that. Maybe if I just ignore him . . .*

Without so much as a glance, I turned and strolled back toward the pickup. The little calf stood with his head tilted way to the other side for a long time, as if trying to figure out why I didn't argue or chase him. When Cookie's mom and Sissy walked away from one another, I sighed and trotted back to the truck.

Kevin patted the place on the tailgate where he'd been sitting. "Hop up, Hoss. Let's head to the house."

I leaped up onto the tailgate, made a couple of circles, and lay down between Ann and Nicole. Kevin reached for Ann.

"Can I ride in the back with Hoss?" She begged. "Pretty please?"

"If Nicole wants to ride with you. And *if* you sit next to the cab."

"We will! We will, won't we, Nicole?" Ann arched her eyebrows.

"Okay. But don't pet Hoss too much. He's all dusty." Nicole crinkled her nose as she herded her sister next to the cab.

The ride to the house was a little bumpy. Ann sat exactly where she was supposed to, but she had a grip on my neck. I held still and didn't even yip when she squeezed a little too tight.

As soon as Kevin stopped the pickup, Nicole jumped out. I hopped down and stood under the tailgate—just in case Ann needed some help or needed something soft (like me) to break her fall. Luckily, Chrissy was there to lift her down.

Once my family was inside, I took off for my lookout spot. This would be a great time for a quick doggie nap. I had just closed my eyes when a smell made my head snap up. I turned my nose toward the breeze and sniffed.

Dog.

No. Two dogs! Hair bristling down my back, I hopped to my feet and looked around. I took about thirty dog-trot paces up the terrace, to a place where I could see across the valley, clear to the edge of our property. When I saw Ree and Pete, our neighbor dogs, my hair flattened and my tail wagged. The two of them were circling a tree about ten yards from their fence line.

I remembered when they'd first come to live with Mr. Park. Kevin had asked him why he named them Ree and Pete. Mr. Park smiled, and told him: "That way I can call both dogs with just one word. Saves time." Kevin had laughed. Mr. Park had laughed.

I didn't get it.

Watching them for a moment or so, I figured they were chasing either a raccoon or a squirrel. Although I couldn't smell which, it didn't take a genius to figure it out. A squirrel. Raccoons are mean and tough. They'll run from you. But if you don't bark and sound mean, when they get tired, they'll turn and pounce right on top of your head. Ree and Pete were circling the tree, taking turns to hop up and put their front paws on the trunk. But they weren't barking. "Yep," I wagged. "Squirrel."

Ree and Pete were good dogs. No threat to our cows. Now was a great time to sneak in that little nap. I settled down and closed my eyes. . . .

A door opened. My head snapped up. Nicole, Ann, and Chrissy were dressed in their nice clothes. Chrissy was carrying a package with bright paper and a ribbon on it. Kevin closed the front door and followed them. I could tell by the clothes they wore that Chrissy and the girls were going to town. Kevin had on his farm clothes, so he was probably going to drive them, then come right back home. While they were away, I had to watch the house, the barn, the cows, the whole place. But since they were just now leaving, I still had a few minutes to close my eyes and—

I didn't even get a chance to lay my chin on

my paws before I heard Rex yipping. It wasn't a "scared" or "danger" yap. He was chasing something. Probably rabbits!

I sprang to my paws and raced off to help.

By the time I reached Chrissy's flower garden, my old pal sat, huffing and puffing under the willow tree. When he glanced up, I perked my ears. "Rabbits?"

"Just one," Rex wheezed. "Smelled like the guy who got into Chrissy's pansies last night. Old stinker . . . must have . . . needed dessert."

Noticing how hard he was gasping for air, I nuzzled him with my snout. "You okay?"

"Fine. Just a little winded."

I glanced over my shoulder. "You stay here and rest. I'll sneak down to the far end of the flower bed and hide. Between the two of us, maybe we can scare them enough so they won't bother you tonight."

Rex nodded his agreement.

Crouching down and with my head low, I started off around the corner of the house.

I'd only gotten about ten paces when the sound of bawling and mooing stopped me dead in my tracks. It grew louder and louder—so loud that even Rex must have heard it above his heavy breathing.

"Better go check that out," he barked.

I hesitated, then turned to face him. "But I promised to help you."

Rex shook his head. "No. Pesky rabbits are *my* job. The cows are *your* job. Go take care of your job. I'm fine."

"You sure?"

"Go!"

I spun and raced off toward the pasture as fast as I could run. I couldn't tell what was wrong. But I could tell it was *serious* trouble!

Chapter 10

A dust cloud rose from the pasture. I could see it even before I topped the hill. The bellowing and bawling was loud and angry. Eyes alert, I stared down at a mass of moving cattle. As the breeze pushed the cloud of dust slowly to the south, I finally saw the problem.

That doggone calf again!

Seven of my ladies stomped and pawed dirt into the air as they made a curved line in front of Cookie. Bellowing and snorting, four of the new cows completed the circle behind him. Head held high, but braced on shaky legs, Cookie stood his ground as the rest of the herd moved in as backup for the others.

If I waited, the cows might charge him. If I

jumped into the middle of that crowd, the cows might turn on me instead.

Several of the older ladies began crowding closer to see what was going on. Cookie's mother, on the edge of the group, just shook her head and mooed softly. Jewel and Sissy were the closest ones to Cookie—standing almost nose to nose with the youngster.

Instead of charging in, stirring everyone up more than they already were, I ambled and wove my way through the cows, cool and calm as could be. Marched straight to Jewel.

"What did he do this time?"

She bobbed her head and gave a little snort without taking her eyes off Cookie. "We've had it with this little calf. He thinks he's the herd bull, but he doesn't have the slightest idea what he's doing."

Cookie pawed another hoof-ful of dirt. The wind lifted it and swirled it around, adding to the already thick dust cloud. "These old cows just won't listen to me," he complained. "They are *not* a good herd. They won't let me protect that mother cow."

I turned to Jewel and perked my ears. "Mother cow?"

"Tess is ready to have her calf," Jewel replied. "She needs to go off by herself. This little know-it-all keeps chasing her back to the herd.

When we try to explain, he becomes extremely rude and tells us we don't know anything."

"Yeah," Sissy chimed in. "*He's* never had a calf. *He* doesn't know anything about being a new mother. Let's get him, ladies."

Before I could blink, five cows started toward Cookie. The calf backed up, but only a step or two. The bigger cows snorted and lowered their heads at him.

Snarling and snapping, I spun in a quick circle. "Sissy! Shut up!" I roared. "The rest of you, back off! I mean it. Stop right where you are."

I knew my ladies well enough to understand that they weren't trying to hurt Cookie. They just wanted this young upstart to leave the mothers alone when they were trying to have their babies. From the corner of my eye I noticed that while the cows kept Cookie's attention, Tess was quietly easing away from the herd. It was all I could do to keep my tail from wagging. If I could only keep him occupied for a few more minutes, just long enough for Tess to make her escape . . .

My ears perked. My nose twitched. Cookie was very protective of his mom.

Quickly, I scanned the herd. Victoria still stood at the edge. Forcing an angry growl to my throat, I started toward her.

When Cookie saw me going after his mother, he instantly charged to get between us. I faked left and went right. Cookie spun and got between us again. This time I faked right and went left. I kept this up until Tess was well out of sight. Then sitting down—with Cookie between us—I cocked my ears at Cookie's mom.

"Victoria. That is your name, isn't it?"

"Yes."

"Victoria, I know you're trying, but maybe you could explain to your son why cows need to be alone when they have their babies. That's really a mother's job, not mine. Besides, I don't exactly know why myself. I just *know,* because I've been around cows for so long. If you had another little chat with him . . . well, all of us would appreciate it, and—"

Kevin's shrill sharp whistle cut me off. Looking around, I spotted him sitting on the four-wheeler by the gate.

He whistled again, even louder than before. "Hoss! Here!" he shouted.

I almost always heard when someone came or left our place. I didn't even hear Kevin come home. And I *always*—and I mean *always*—heard the four-wheeler. Next to bacon, it was one of my favorite things. I guess I was so busy with that stupid calf, I hadn't heard. Tail tucked and head down—to let Kevin know how ashamed I was for not coming sooner—I raced to him.

"What are you doin', mutt? Think I'm running a taxi service? You want to ride the four-wheeler, you got to come to me. I'm not driving down to the pasture and opening two gates just to pick up your furry tail." He ruffled the hair on top of my head, then turned to thump the platform on the back of the four-wheeler. "Hop up."

Made of metal pipe, the platform was for carrying stuff—not dogs. So Kevin had put a piece of wood over the pipes. That way my paws wouldn't fall through the gaps. The wood was tied down with wire, but it was a little slippery for my nails, so he had tacked a piece of carpet on top of the wood. That way, I had something to hold on to.

I hopped up, made two quick circles, plopped my rump on the rug, and leaned my head over Kevin's shoulder. He shrugged, giving my chin a little bump. "I know you love riding this thing," he chuckled, "but back off. I don't want you slobbering on me all the way down the road." With that, he revved the motor, and off we went.

I loved the way the wind blew in my face. It made my ears wiggle. It made my jowls flop and pop and jiggle. Just the fresh air blowing in my nostrils was enough to make my head spin with delight.

We whizzed down the driveway and turned left. My tail thumped the carpet. We were headed to Meme Kay's and Papa John's farm. The bigger calves were on their place. It was about three sections from us. That meant I got to ride, with the wind in my face, for three whole miles.

Meme Kay and Papa John were retired.

At least I think that's what Kevin called them. It meant that they didn't farm or raise cattle, because they were old and couldn't work as hard as they used to. Since they weren't using their farm, Kevin and Chrissy rented it.

Our second herd was there, and it was time to bring them to the lot to give them their shots and pour some kind of liquid on their backs that would keep the flies away.

I could hardly wait to stop at the house and let Kevin's mom and dad know we were there. Meme Kay always had some snacks or doggie-treats. And if I was *really* lucky, Papa John would have some oatmeal cookies. Between the wind blowing in my face and the thought of those delicious cookies, my tail thumped all the way there.

We didn't stop at the house.

Bummer.

Instead, we went straight to the pasture. That was okay, too. The sooner we got the cattle to the lot, the sooner we could go see Meme and Papa.

Naturally, the herd was at the far end of the farm. That meant Kevin and I would have to drive them about a mile or so to get them into the lot near the house. Kevin started them moving with the four-wheeler. My job was to help. There were always some who tried to hide in the trees along the creeks, or the big plum patches on the hill.

The four-wheeler couldn't go there, so I had to chase them out and keep them moving with the rest of the herd. It was hard work. I'd be doing a lot of running and a lot of barking.

Two trips later, I was plumb tuckered out. The first run, Kevin and I got most of them in the lot. Papa John was there to shut the gate. But right before they went in, this one heifer bolted. She was almost as kookie as Cookie. She jumped right over Kevin *and* the four-wheeler. Two steers and three heifers raced after her. They ran clear to the far end of the big pasture before they stopped. Kevin had me hop on my seat, and he drove us back to where we started.

The six youngsters were tired. It was pretty easy to bring them up the second time. But I was so exhausted, my tongue was almost dragging the ground. Papa John made sure there was plenty of water in the trough.

"When's the vet coming?" he called to Kevin.

"What?" Kevin asked, as he came from the barn with a bale of hay. "Couldn't hear you."

"When is the vet coming?" Papa John repeated.

Kevin hoisted the bale over the fence, then climbed over and cut the wire with his pliers. "Thought we'd give 'em a couple of days to settle down. Think Tony's gonna come and help, too."

Papa John nodded. "Sounds good to me.

Let's leave them alone. Come on to the house. Just made a fresh batch of cookies."

A cool dip in the cattle trough and three oatmeal cookies later, I felt great. The ride home was better than getting to come inside during the summer and sit in front of the air conditioner.

Once we were back at the house, Kevin went inside and changed into his good clothes. When he drove off, I made my way to the terrace, where I could see most of our farm. My herd seemed to be doing fine. It took me a second or two to find Cookie. He was wandering around, not far from where I'd left him earlier. He was all by himself. His head was only an inch or two above the ground. He was sniffing the grass, as if hunting for something.

The area he searched was the last place I'd seen Tess. I guess he was still trying to find her so he could chase her back to the rest of the herd. He finally raised his head and trotted off toward the east. Lucky for me and for Cookie, cows can't smell as well as us dogs. He was headed the opposite direction from where Tess had gone. Still, it was probably a good idea to go check and see if she was okay.

I circled near the house, crossed the creek, then climbed to the playhouse on the ridge. Careful not to be seen or heard, I eased my way to the edge of the big flat rock.

Tess was grazing in the open area off to my right. Three cedar trees gave her the privacy she wanted, and she was a good distance from the canyon to my left. A mother bobcat had a den and a litter of cubs up in that canyon about five years ago. After her cubs were big enough to walk on their own, Rex and I convinced her to move. She hadn't been back since, but I always got a little nervous when my ladies went too near the canyon to have their calves.

Once sure that Tess was fine, I headed back to my lookout spot on the terrace. I had just sat down when Kevin and Chrissy came outside and loaded the girls in the pickup. I guess they came back while I was checking our herd. They didn't call for me, so I figured there wasn't any work that needed to be done. When they left, they headed toward town again. While they were gone, I needed to keep an eye on things.

My herd was barely in view from where I sat on the terrace. I checked them first, to make sure the new calves were okay. Then I patrolled around the house and barn, found Cookie, to make sure he wasn't causing any problems, then started all over again with Tess.

So much for my nap.

Chapter 11

It was a little after dark when my family came home. They smelled like popcorn. I knew the smell because they made popcorn at home a few times. They even let me taste it. Not that I cared for it all that much. And I never could figure out why they got all dressed up and went to town to eat something they could make right here at the house. It just didn't make sense. 'Course, there were a lot of things people did that didn't make sense.

Chrissy fed Rex and me. No scraps or yummies, just dry food. When we were done, Rex and I headed for Chrissy's garden. She had all sorts of stuff planted across the front and down the east side of the house. The rabbits didn't mess with her flower garden very much until fall. During the spring and early summer, Rex had to patrol the vegetable garden out back of the house almost all the time. If he didn't, some of the corn and most all of the green beans would disappear. Rabbits loved the new bean sprouts.

In the fall, it was different. Although the pesky rabbits didn't like the berries that grew on the barberry shrubs, they loved to nibble the bright gold and red leaves. Both the barberry bushes and the bush sunflowers grew in a line close to the house. In front of them were Chrissy's petunias, two patches of blackberries, and one patch of raspberries. The rabbits didn't seem to bother the leaves or stems on those, but they loved the little white flowers and the berries. That's what made Rex and me mad.

When Chrissy worked in her garden, Nicole and Ann loved to sit near the berry patches and munch on the ripe blackberries. If the rabbits ate the flowers, there were no berries. They liked the berries, too. So if they got to either one before our girls did, there were none left. And that made both Rex and me . . . well, it made us *really* mad.

Rex and I trotted around to the front of the house. "You want to herd and chase," I asked, "or do you want to work the ambush?"

Rex shrugged his ears. "Why don't we let the rabbits decide?"

My head drew back, just a little. My ears perked. "Huh?"

"They usually come from the pasture in front of the house or from the east side. When I chase one or two far enough so they don't want to come back, another sneaks in while I'm gone. If I don't chase them far enough, they come right back while I'm running after another one."

"In other words, they're double-teaming you?"

"Right," he answered with a curled lip and a flash of his sharp teeth. "If they come from the front, I'll chase. Two barks means they're heading in your direction. Get ready to ambush. One bark means they've turned back toward the front pasture and I'll keep chasing while you move up so you can watch both directions. You do the same for me if they come from the east side of the house."

I nodded. "Two barks if they're coming toward your ambush. One bark if they're headed back to the east. Got it."

Rex trotted to the corner of the house. He plopped down, and all I could see was the tip of his nose. The rest of him was hidden by the wall. I trotted to the back of the house and lay down so I could just see the east side. One of Chrissy's sunflowers was right at that edge of the house. It gave me a great hiding place.

It took less than ten minutes for the first rabbit to show up. My keen ears heard Rex running.

Then he barked twice. That meant the rabbit was coming in my direction.

Every muscle tensed, but I didn't move. The rabbit finally came into view through the leaves of my bush sunflower. Long ears flat against his back, he was running hard—only about four feet from the rock edge of Chrissy's garden. My muscles tightened even more. Every nerve ending tingled. Still, I forced myself not to move until . . . the last second.

When he was close enough, I sprang. While still in midair, I let out my loudest, most ferocious growl. Teeth bared, jaws gaping wide, I landed smack-dab in front of him.

Rabbits are really good at dodging and turning. But I timed my ambush perfectly. He was so close, he didn't stand a chance. He *tried* to dart to the right. Instead, he slipped—fell and slid on his side. He clunked right into my left paw. Towering above him, I leaned down. Roared again. Snapped my powerful jaws just inches from his face.

Dumb bunny didn't run off!

His little legs were still churning like mad. But lying on his side, he wasn't going anyplace. I leaned down and snapped again. The little feet ran faster, but he still wasn't going anyplace.

Then Rex was there!

He roared. He opened his huge jaws. He leaned down, snapped them shut like a coyote trap, and . . .

. . . got hold of the very tip of the rabbit's little fuzzy, bunny tail.

When Rex raised his head, the rabbit had his running feet once more. He took off like a shot—leaving just a little fur between Rex's teeth. We both barked and bounced off after him. But we took only a couple of bounces. The rabbit was halfway to the pasture before we took our third bounce. He ran square into the big post at the corner of the fence. The impact sent him tumbling backward. He rolled twice, got to his feet, darted under the barbed wire (missing the post this time), and disappeared into the tall grass.

Rex and I had our lips curled back far enough that our gums were showing. Our tails were wagging so hard and fast, we were whacking each other on the rump.

When we finally quit laughing—got our lips unstuck from our teeth—I sat and looked at Rex. "Okay. You've known for a long time that I don't like the taste of rabbit. Ain't too crazy about all that hair, either. But I thought you liked 'em. I thought you were gonna take a mouthful of him just now. What's the deal?"

Rex shrugged his ears. "Used to like the taste of them when I was younger. Now they just give me gas."

We took a second or two to watch where the grass was parting, far out in the pasture. Then Rex hopped to his feet. "Don't reckon that one will be back." He wagged. "Let's see if we can scare another."

Rex circled behind the house to his hiding place. I returned to my spot next to the bush sunflower. About twenty minutes later, I chased one to Rex. A while after that, I spotted another. Only this one went straight to the pasture. While I was out in the grass following him, sure enough, another rabbit came. I could hear Rex barking. All in all, we ambushed about five of the pesky little suckers and chased off four more. Working together, the two of us did such a good job that within a couple of hours there was nothing left to chase. We settled down for a good night's sleep.

Only . . . I didn't sleep that well. Every time I closed my eyes, I kept thinking about that doggone calf and wondering what he was going to do next.

The sun came up a lot sooner than I expected, so I guess I really did get some shuteye. Still, I felt restless.

Now that it was light, the rabbits usually stayed in the safety of their burrows. I told Rex I'd check on him later, then left to do my morning rounds. My family was quiet. "Must still be asleep," I snorted.

The barn was secure. Well, I did hear one rat trying to gnaw through the metal bin where Kevin kept the sweet feed sacks for the cows. I couldn't get inside the barn to chase him, but that was all right. The metal was so thick, he'd never chew through it. Besides, our three barn cats would take care of him if he kept gnawing and making noise. Next I decided to check on Tess.

I crept across the big flat rock at the playhouse and peeked over the edge. Tess had had her new baby. He must have come just moments before I got there. He was still wet, and Tess was cleaning him with her tongue. He wasn't quite ready to stand on his wobbly legs yet. I waited until he was up, then headed for my lookout spot.

I didn't even make a circle or two before lying down. Fact is, I plopped so hard that it almost knocked the air out of me. My eyes closed the instant I landed, and I was sound asleep within seconds.

Chapter 12

The sound of bawling made my eyes open. I left my lookout spot and headed for the pasture in front of the house. Rex was still asleep on the porch. He needed his rest.

Although I had a good idea who was bawling, I couldn't see past the row of Johnson grass that grew in the fence line. Once under the fence and through the grass, it didn't take me long to spot who was making the racket. It wasn't any big surprise, either.

Cookie was trying to moo. Trouble was, his voice hadn't changed yet. His "moo" sounded more like a calf bawling. I sat down to watch and listen. Sure enough—he was calling for Tess. Still trying to find her.

All I could do was shake my head. *Well, at least he's not bothering any of our ladies,* I thought. *He's not close enough to the house to wake Rex or the family.* I shrugged my ears and headed back to the porch. I thought I heard a door close, but Rex was still on the porch and not inside eating breakfast. *Must be hearing things,* I thought.

Trying to make sure Rex wouldn't be disturbed, I decided not to hop up. Instead, I took the steps. I was only on the second one when I saw the old dog watching me out of one eye. He wiggled a whisker, twitched his upper lip, and raised an eyebrow to ask, "Cookie?"

"Cookie," I answered. "If he gets any louder, I'll chase him clean off our place. You think he's just scared. I think he's got to be the most stubborn animal I ever met in my whole life."

Rex's tail thumped the porch. "I remember someone who was just as bad, if not worse."

I lowered my head. Looked at him out of the tops of my eyes. "Worse scared? Or worse stubborn?"

"Both."

I thought for a second. "Nicole?" I figured that was a good guess. Every time I complained about stuff Ann did, Rex had a worse story about Nicole.

"Nope."

"Ann?"

"Nope."

I had to think a minute. "Jewell, 'cause when she was young, she's the one who cracked your hip?"

"Nope."

"Then who?"

"Go look in the pond." Rex's tail thumped even louder. "You'll see him."

"There's nobody in the pond but fish. They're not stubborn—they're just fish. Who are you talking about?"

"You'll recognize him when you see him." Rex's tail twitched. "He's got pointed ears. He's big, strong, young—a German shepherd, just like you." With that Rex rolled over on his back. His tail whipped so hard that it made his feet kick the air. I thought he was going to laugh himself off the porch.

"That's not a real dog," I growled. "That's my face looking back at me. It's a . . . a . . . It's a refexion."

"Reflection," Rex snapped, struggling to his feet. "I told you that. But every time you saw that dog looking up at you, you'd whimper and take off—either run to me or to the house. You were so scared of yourself, the only way I could get you to drink was to stand in the water and make ripples. That way you wouldn't see 'the dog.'

"Then one day you finally got tired of being scared. You snarled, and growled, and pounced right on that dog. Bit a whole mouthful of water before I could get there."

"So what's your point?"

"The point is, first off you had to quit being scared. Second, you had to learn—or figure it out for yourself. That bull calf is scared. He's in a new place. People yelled at him. You chased him. I think he's a good calf. He wants to be herd bull, but he's scared he won't know how. He just needs time to quit being scared. Best thing you can do is give him some time. Quit chasing him and growling at him. If you try to help him . . . well, maybe it might work better than threatening him all the time."

The sound of a metal gate clanking stopped Rex just as he stretched his leg. We both glanced toward the corral.

In the distance, Cookie wiggled his ears, swished at a fly with his tail, then lowered his head and charged the gate.

Nobody tears up the gates, I thought. *Not on my watch.*

Cookie managed to butt the gate two more times before I got there. I raced up behind him—just out of range of his hooves—and slid to a stop. "What are you doing now, you bloomin' idiot?"

Sure enough, he kicked. I was far enough away that his sharp little hoof didn't even come close. He glared at me, then lowered his head once more.

Clunk!

"Hey, kid, knock it off!" I growled. "You're gonna bend Kevin's gate. What are you doing?"

"Tess hasn't returned to the herd. I've looked everyplace. She must be in here or hiding in that big thing on the hill." He lowered his head again.

Clank!

I raced to the gate, slipped under, and came up snapping at his nose. "I mean it, Cookie. Back away from the gate or I'm gonna—"

"What did you call me?" he demanded suddenly, standing very tall and straight.

"Cookie. I'm serious. You better—"

"My name is *not* Cookie. My name is Sir Winston Berkshire of—"

"*I don't care!*" I roared. "Nicole and Ann call you Cookie. So as far as I'm concerned—"

"Ann calls me that?"

I nodded. "Yes. Now, get away from that gate, or I swear I'm gonna—"

"If she calls me Cookie, then you are allowed to refer to me by that name as well. Now, move, dog. I don't wish to hurt you when I break through this gate."

My lips curled to a snarl. *Chasing him and threatening him hadn't worked worth a flip . . .*

I forced my lips down to cover my teeth once more. *Rex was always giving me advice. I didn't really care for most of it. I was old enough and smart enough to make my own decisions. But maybe . . . just maybe . . .*

I wagged my tail when I leaned my head through the bars of the gate. "Cookie . . . Tess isn't in the pens. She isn't in the 'big thing up there,' which, by the way, is called a barn."

Cookie snorted and pawed the ground. "You've hidden her! It is my right to see my cows. I demand to know where she is!"

My eyes felt like they spun around in my head a couple of times. *Crazy little . . .* "Look, kid. Just relax. She'll probably be back to the herd today, or early tomorrow. Just be patient and—"

"Mother said she would come back one or two days after she had her baby. She should be back today. She hasn't returned. There must be something wrong, and it's my right to know what has happened to—"

"Hold on. Hold on." I hopped up and placed my front paws on the rail he kept butting. "Cows don't always have their calves the first day they leave the herd. Tess didn't have her calf until early this morning. They're both doing fine, and she'll probably come back soon—just like I said."

Cookie stomped a hoof and snorted. He blew so hard that little drops showered at me and clung to my whiskers and fur. "I knew it! You've hidden her. I demand to see her, right this instant!" With that, he lunged at the gate once more.

I jerked my paws out of the way just in the nick of time. "Look, kid! You keep buttin' that gate, Kevin's gonna hear and come to see what's going on. If you end up bending the thing, then this week or next, when he and Tony sort the young ones—you're *gone!*"

Cookie frowned and tilted his head. "Gone?"

"Yes. Gone! Like 'gone to market.'"

"What does that mean?"

"It means—"

All of a sudden, my eyes flashed so wide, I felt like my eyeballs were going to pop out. *I can't believe I said that,* I thought. *"Gone" was just something we didn't talk about with the cows— especially the younger ones, like Cookie.*

"What does 'gone to market,' mean," he insisted.

Talk about "Open mouth, insert paw . . ."

I sighed and shook my head until my ears flopped. "It means . . . uh . . . well, it's just a place . . . and . . . uh . . ." I stammered. "It's not a bad place, really . . . and it's . . . well, no, it *is* a bad place, but . . . but . . ."

You just don't talk about going to market with a cow. You don't mention things like hamburger or steaks or rump roast. I felt so bad that if I could have found a big rock to crawl under, I would have curled right up and died.

I didn't know how I was *ever* going to get out of this one.

Chapter 13

"Why don't you show him where Tess is?"

The sudden smell and soft whimper that came from behind me made me spin to see who was there. Rex had his head down, showing his disappointment at what I had done. I could barely see his eyes under his eyebrows. I lowered my head to let him know how sorry I was.

Rex nodded and straightened a bit. I could tell he was upset with me—although probably no more than I was with myself. I could also tell he was trying to help. "Go ahead," he urged. "Show him where Tess and her calf are, so he'll know they're all right."

If nothing else, I thought, *it would give me some time. Take the little guy's mind off "gone to market" long enough for me to figure out a way to explain, a way to tell him without lying. Cows aren't as smart as us dogs . . . but they can smell a lie just as easily as we can. Maybe it would give me time to figure out what to say. And maybe— just maybe—I could help him out some while I was at it.*

I gave Rex a quick flip of one ear to thank him for his help. Then I turned to Cookie.

"I'll take you to them. But"—I stuck my nose through the gate and pressed it right against the little calf's nose—"you have to listen to what I say. Got it?"

He didn't answer. He just stared, cross-eyed, at the point where our noses met.

"Got it?" I repeated.

He blinked. "Got it."

I slipped under the metal gate to Cookie's side of the fence. Then, with him right on my heels, we headed for the pasture. "First off, you're always complaining that you should have the 'right' to do things because of your papers, because you're 'royalty'—whatever that means— or because your grandfather was champion of something in some place we've never heard of. This is a working ranch. Your papers may be important where you come from, but they don't mean squat here. On this ranch, you don't have rights because of who your parents were. You have to *earn* your rights. You have to do your job. And the most important thing that you haven't figured out yet is that with each privilege, there is more responsibility."

"If I am to be herd bull, what *is* my job?"

"Your main job will be to help your herd make calves."

"How do I do that?"

That stopped me! I turned and looked up at him.

"Ah . . . well, when you get a little older, you'll know. But if you don't stay around here for more than a week or two, you'll *never* be the herd bull."

"I'll be 'gone to market,' right?"

I cleared my throat, turned, and trotted on. "Right. Market is a place you *really* don't want to go. You can't be herd bull if you go there. The people aren't nice, and . . . well, I guarantee that you'll be a lot happier if you get to stay here. Trouble is, if you don't start being responsible, you won't stay!"

"What does res—respon—whatever that word was . . . what does it mean?"

"Responsible?"

"Yes. That word."

"Being responsible means . . . ah . . . well, doing what you're supposed to do. Doing the things that need to be done, whether you want to do them or not. *And* not doing the things you shouldn't do."

"Such as?"

"Such as—well, you don't butt the gates or tear up the fences. You don't chase people, especially Chrissy or the girls. You don't act wild and crazy by running around the pens or crashing into the corral. You don't get the cows all stirred up by trying to boss them around or chasing one of the mamas back to the herd when she's trying to go off and have her calf. And when you check on one of the new mamas and her calf, you don't scare them or startle them. They need their time alone."

We were halfway up the hill when I stopped. "Now, Tess is just over this hill. When we get there . . ."

Cookie trotted on ahead of me. I chased after him.

"Stop!" I growled. To my surprise, he stopped. "Stay behind me," I told him. "The key to checking on your cows is to *not* let them know you're watching. We're going to go up the hill, real quiet. The second you see Tess, stop. We're not going to let her know we're around. We won't scare her, or make any noise, or try to chase her back to the herd. All we're going to do is look. Okay?"

Cookie was amazing! He followed me up the rock hill quiet as could be. At the playhouse, he stayed behind me as we crept across the flat rock. When he stomped his big heavy hoof, I turned to see what he wanted.

"Why do they call it the playhouse?"

I explained how Kevin used to come here to play when he was little. How Nicole and Ann liked to come here with him. And even about chasing Ann down and grabbing her by the pants, afraid that she might fall over the edge. He gave a little snort and nodded. We moved on.

Suddenly, Cookie stopped. I'd forgotten how much taller he was than I. He was a good five doggie paces behind me, but because of his height, he could see things I couldn't. Watching his eyes to see where he was looking, I figured he had spotted Tess. I moved forward until I could see her, too.

"When I was just a young pup," I whispered, "I trotted up through the cedar trees one time to see how one of our cows was doing. She hadn't had her calf yet, but she charged me. Ran me halfway back to the house. Never did figure out where she finally went to be alone. But a couple of days later, she and a little heifer showed up with the herd again."

"I saw two coyotes yesterday evening," Cookie said. "How about them? Do I need to run the coyotes off?"

"There are a lot of coyotes around. They usually don't harm the calves. Mostly, they eat grasshoppers, field mice, and rabbits. They're smart animals. They know if a mama cow kicks them or tromps on them, they're gonna get hurt. If they're hurt, they can't hunt or catch food.

"The big problem is dogs. People dump their dogs. Not many, just the dumb people—the ones who don't have any heart. A few dumped dogs—*very* few—find a home. Most starve to death. The ones who do learn how to find food are the ones you have to watch out for. Dogs aren't afraid of people, or other dogs. Wild pack dogs are a lot more dangerous than any old coyote."

"What do you do if one of my mama cows has difficulty having her baby?" Cookie asked.

I shrugged my ears. "Not much you can do. Kevin's really good about checking on our cows. If a cow is having a problem, he usually takes care of it. If he can't handle it, he calls that place called 'the Vet,' and someone comes out to help. Guess the cows know that Kevin and people are there to help."

To my surprise, Cookie seemed to be listening, paying attention to what I was telling him. Once he was sure Tess and her baby were all right, we backed away.

"Is this the only place they go to have their babies?" Cookie asked.

Then, I took him to the wide place on the edge of the creek. There was a big opening in the trees, and it was well above the water. The grass was short but thick. It made the perfect place. I explained that if he didn't come crashing through the trees, or sloshing in the water, he could get close enough to check on them without being noticed.

Next we went to the plum thicket on the hill. Sneaking up on this place was a little harder. So I showed Cookie where the "thin" spot was—a place where some of the old plum bushes had died and the new ones hadn't taken over. "If you stay close to the fence, you can see clear to the middle of the thicket from here. Just don't get too close."

"I will do my best not to disturb the mother cows, farm dog, but—"

"You can call me Hoss."

"—but," he repeated, "it is my res—respon— what was that word again?"

"Responsibility?"

He nodded. "Yeah, that's it. I have a res-pons-o-bilily to do."

"Responsibility," I corrected.

"Responsibility," he repeated. "I appreciate your assistance. Thank you very much." With that, he turned and headed down the hill.

"There are a couple of other spots I can show you. What's the rush?"

When he didn't answer, I trotted to his side. "Wait—what's the hurry?"

He glanced at me but didn't slow down. "I

have a responsibilily to Ann. She comes out early to pet me before the other people wake. I should have already been there. Being with her is my responsibilily. Please excuse me."

His trot quickened. I stood with my mouth gaping and my head tilted so far to one side, my ear almost touched the ground. *Ann? Sneaking off from the house to pet Cookie? Impossible! Surely, I would have noticed. How could I miss hearing or smelling Ann if she left?*

"Hey, hang on a second, Cookie!" I barked, racing after him. "Hold up. How long has this petting stuff been going on? What's the deal with you and Ann? And how does she leave the house without Chrissy or Kevin knowing? And how—"

I never finished what I was trying to ask.

We were a ways past the creek—about halfway between there and the house—when a smell tugged at my nose. A dog. Probably Rex. I was so busy trying to catch up with Cookie that for an instant I didn't pay it much attention. Not until another scent came. Two dogs. They weren't Rex. They weren't Ree and Pete, either. Then there was a third odor.

Three dogs!

Hungry dogs!

I spun and trotted back to where I had first noticed the smell. Then I followed it. Three dogs. Two about my size, judging by the paw prints and the scent. The third dog's track was big—his smell was heavy and strong. All three were headed toward the cedar trees.

The cedar trees below the playhouse cliff.

The cedar trees where Tess and her new baby were.

Chapter 14

"Tess needs us," I barked. "Her baby might need help."

I'm pretty sure Cookie didn't hear me. I was already running in the opposite direction. I didn't have time to chase after him.

Maybe I'm wrong, I thought. *Maybe those dogs are just passing across our place and don't even smell Tess or her calf.* But that thought didn't linger long. The dogs' trails made a beeline straight for the cedars.

The sound of barking caught my ear. Then I heard Tess. Her moo was deep in her throat. Not scared or hurt—it was more like a growl, a warning to leave her baby alone. I raced through the brush, dodged around the big sunflower stalks, and hopped over the tangled peavine that might catch my paws and slow me down.

The barking and threats grew louder as I neared the three trees. Cautiously, I slowed. The noise seemed closer to the opening of the canyon than to the cedar. I eased beside the first tree.

Tess stood near the mouth of the canyon, tossing her head at a yellow dog. He had long legs and a lean body. Probably a mix between a greyhound and something. Sizing him up, I figured I could take him in a one-on-one fight. But there was no way I could outrun him. Not with those legs. A few feet beyond him was a shaggy dog with long matted hair. She had a coonhound's ears and build, but her coat looked more like a mix between a collie and a sheepdog. She was more of a danger than the yellow dog. Not only was she bigger than the yellow dog, but if she attacked, she'd be harder to get a hold of through that thick, matted coat.

I couldn't find the third dog.

Moving around the cedar, I came out on the far side. I checked the other two trees to make sure the third dog wasn't hiding near them, then eased forward, one step at a time.

When you're outnumbered three to one, it's always a good idea to know where *all* your attackers might come from. But three to one wasn't quite right.

Tess was a good cow, calm and sweet most of the time. But now she was one mad mama!

Right now she was protecting her baby. Even trying to help her, if I got too close, or tangled with one of the dogs within her range, she'd stomp both of us into the dirt. Either that or grind us to mush with her hard head and short horns. Sure, she'd feel sorry about it afterward, when she realized it was me and I'd only come to help. She'd feel really bad. But if I got in her way, that wouldn't help me—not one little bit.

If I got too close to Tess, I'd be outnumbered four to one. I sure wished Rex was here to help. That would cut the odds. Without him, I had only two things going for me. First off, I knew cows. I knew not to get too close to Tess. Second, I knew dogs—at least, how they thought and hunted.

The big dog with the matted coat and the greyhound were "runners." Their job was to keep the cow busy—to draw her away from the calf. They had to get close enough so she would chase them and, at the same time, not so close that they'd get stomped. With each charge, bark, and growl, they were testing her. Seeing how quick she was, how far she would go away from her calf. How close they had to let her get to them to keep her from breaking off the chase and turning back. Once they knew her range and how fast or slow she moved, one or both would draw her off.

The third member of the pack—the one I still couldn't find—was the "kill dog." It had to be close, but not too close—nearby and hidden, so it could race in, get the calf, and then get away before Tess came back.

My eyes darted from one place to the next. Not under the cedars. Not behind the big rock to the left of the canyon. Tangle-vines and wild grapes on the right side of the canyon—not there, either.

Glancing back to make sure it wasn't sneaking up behind me, I moved away from the tree and drew closer to Tess. Still no sign of the kill dog. I stopped. I forced my eyes to slow, to focus instead of darting around. I searched every rock, shadow, clump of grass, pile of brush. I didn't blink . . . didn't move . . . didn't even breathe.

It wasn't my eyes that found the dog.

There was a noise. A rock. It clattered, tumbled, and bounced against other stones as it toppled from the spot where something had knocked it loose. My ears homed in on the sound. My eyes followed upward.

At the middle of the far hill I could see a large male. He must have circled way around and was planning to come up behind Tess—slip down from the hill and attack her calf while she was busy with the other two dogs. He stood totally still until the rock stopped making noise. When he saw that Tess didn't turn toward the sound, he took another step or two.

He was *huge*!

The Rottweiler was black with brown eyebrows. When I saw his size and build, my front paws tried to back up. But my hind paws wouldn't let them.

Tess needs help, I growled. *I can't run. I have to do something. Maybe if I could let Tess know he's there . . . maybe if I can turn her . . . the two of us together could . . .*

For just an instant, I studied the distance between the enormous dog and the baby calf. *If I could get past the yellow dog and start barking, Tess would turn on me. Maybe then she would see the big dog.* My tail gave a little wag. *Yeah, that just might work. If she sees me, she'll turn and see the third dog, too.*

I glanced back to the Rott. He was on the move again. One step at a time, sneaking up, quietly on the . . . on the . . .

He wasn't watching the calf. He wasn't even looking in that direction.

He was stalking something else.

I tried to follow the path of his eyes. His eyes were staring at something across the canyon. No, it was the playhouse rock. I studied his eyes once more. A place farther down the hill. Down and to the left a little from the playhouse, and—

My eyes flashed when I saw where he was staring.

The breath caught in my throat.

My heart stopped.

Chapter 15

"**B**ad dogs! You leave our cow alone." Ann's eyes squinted to narrow slits. Her chin jutted out, and her cheeks were bright red. White knuckles clutched a small, flimsy stick. She shook it at the two dogs. "Bad, bad dogs!"

Without a thought, I bolted—charged across the flat between the cedars and the rocks at the base of the hill.

Normally, dogs never attack people. But from the smell of them, from the look of them, from watching the way they moved, these weren't "normal" dogs. They were hungry. Starving. They were so hungry, they would eat anything they could. Anything.

I glanced at Ann.

Anything!

The word seemed to echo inside my head. It made my fur quiver from the tip of my tail to the bridge of my snout.

I had to get to my Ann!

The two runners were so busy with Tess, neither of them heard or saw me. I knew I couldn't handle the Rott, but one-on-one was still better than two against one.

I was halfway to Ann when I heard a sound behind me. Nails scratching against rock. Loose gravel clicking, clattering down the slope. I didn't look back. I didn't slow. But my ears turned, trying to home in on the noise. It had to be the yellow dog. He was gaining on me. But not too close yet.

Glancing across the canyon, I found the huge Rott. He was just starting down the edge of the slope on the far side. It would take him a few seconds to reach the bottom, then more time to cross the wide part of the canyon and start up the playhouse side.

Never taking his eyes from Ann, he licked his slobbery lips. He seemed to move faster, the farther he made it down the slope.

The sound behind me was close. I ran harder, leaped from one rock to anther, dodged around the bigger boulders. Once more I glanced to see where the big guy was. He was halfway down the slope now. Even from far away, he looked enormous. The best I could hope for was to keep him busy long enough for Ann to get away. But if that yellow dog caught up with me . . . neither Ann nor I would have a chance.

I sucked in a deep breath. Ran even faster than I thought my legs could carry me. The yellow dog was closer now. If I stopped here, he could circle out of my reach and get—

I had to get to Ann!

The yellow dog was right behind me—no more than four or five strides. I could hear his breathing. About two yards from Ann, I stopped, spun, lowered my head, and charged!

The yellow dog's eyes flashed wide. Running as fast as he was, those long legs didn't give him time to dodge. When I lunged, I caught him square under the chin. The instant I felt the impact on the top of my head, I lunged a second time. Only this time, I lifted upward.

I was heavier than he was, and I was coming up underneath him. The impact flipped him over on his back. Snarling and growling, I leaped on top of him, roaring as fierce and angry as I could. He wriggled loose, but only bounded about three or four jumps. Then he turned to come after me again. Before he had a chance to move, I leaped on him a second time.

Tangled up, we both rolled down the hill. He snapped at me but missed. I snapped back, getting a hold on the scruff of his neck. I guess I also got a tooth or two in an ear. He yapped and squealed. When we stopped tumbling, he leaped to his feet.

This time he didn't turn back. Tail tucked, he raced off, clear to the bottom of the hill.

My tail wagged. Nine times out of ten, if one dog in a pack takes off hurt, the others will follow. As soon as I knew he was gone, I hurried to Ann.

She was still waving the little stick in her hand like a club. I saw two tears trickling down her cheeks.

"You leave Hoss alone!" Her voice quivered when she screamed. "You hurt my Hoss again, I'll paddle your bottom!"

She petted my head and stroked my back when I stopped beside her. I looked down the hill. The yellow dog was still running. The girl dog, with the matted hair, was backing away from Tess. She took off in the direction of the yellow dog, then stopped. Her head twisted back and forth, from one side to the other, as if she was trying to decide whether to run or stay.

If she ran, then that enormous Rott wouldn't stick around, either. Even a starving dog knows that without his runners he can't take on a mad mama cow alone. I looked toward the hill on the other side of the canyon. I couldn't see him. When I started to go look over the edge, Ann wrapped her arms around my neck.

"I love you, Hoss," she sniffed. "I don't want that mean old dog to hurt you. You stay away from those nasty, stinky doggies. If they come back, I'll hit them with my club."

But I had to know where the big dog was. Flattening my ears and stretching my neck, I tried to slip out of Ann's grasp. She only tightened her hold.

If the Rott was running away with the others, he wouldn't go down the floor of the canyon. That would be too close to Tess. So I should be able to see him on the far hill, backtracking the way he came. But he wasn't there.

I tried to slip away from Ann once more. Still scared, she squeezed my neck so hard, I could barely breathe.

I didn't want to hurt her, I didn't want to knock her down or have her scrape her knee on the rock. But I had to know!

With a sigh, I let out all of my breath and relaxed. When I felt her grip loosen, I yanked backward and slipped out. Before she could hug me again, I scampered to the side of the canyon.

The Rott wasn't on the far hill. I looked to the floor of the canyon, toward Tess and her calf.

No dog.

Leaning forward, I looked down the side of the cliff where I stood.

Nothing.

Suddenly, a noise. A paw appeared. It was right under my nose—the nails almost touching my nails. Then a second paw. My hair bristled, clear from my ears to the tip of my tail. I heard a grunt, then hind paws scratching on loose rocks. Another grunt.

Suddenly, a humongous head appeared—right below me. On the very rock where I stood. Black eyes glared up at me. Then, startled to see another dog this close, they popped wide.

I did the only thing I could. I barked . . . growled . . . leaned over and nipped his big fat ugly snout.

That startled him even more. He yipped. Lost his hold on the rock.

There was a loud thump when he landed right on his little fat stubbed tail. The instant he hit, he tumbled backward. A whole lot of clunking and crashing and rocks clacking together followed him as he tumbled down the cliff to the flat part of the canyon. By the time he and the rocks stopped bouncing around, my tail was wagging so hard, it kept hitting me in the sides.

Like I said, I could not take this guy in a fight. He was too big, too strong. It was just sheer dumb luck that saved both Ann and me. After taking a fall like that, he had to be pretty well scratched up, pretty sore. There was no way he was gonna come back for more. He'd take off with those other two dogs and—

The other two!

I looked over my right shoulder. The bigger dog, with the matted hair, was making her way back up the hill. I really don't think she'd spotted Ann yet. But she hadn't run off. She was coming to see what all the commotion was about or to see where her giant friend was. The yellow dog wasn't far behind. I leaned forward and looked down at the Rott.

When he looked back at me, it sent a chill skittering up my back. His eyes were tight. His stare black as death. Even from where I was, I could feel his hate and anger cut right into me. He struggled to his feet. Those angry eyes never left mine as he started once more up the canyon wall toward Ann and me.

The strong paws clawed and ripped rocks from his path as he climbed the steep slope even faster than before.

Chapter 16

I rushed to Ann. There was no way down, because two dogs were coming from that direction. They were moving slow—more cautious but still hungry. Hungry for anything.

Anything!

The word echoed inside my head again.

We couldn't stay here.

That was one furious mutt climbing toward us. The only chance we had was to get to the playhouse. And that was a long shot.

We wouldn't be safe there, either, unless Chrissy or Kevin had noticed that Ann was missing. If Chrissy remembered the last time Ann sneaked away from the house, they'd check the creek first. Then they would come to the playhouse.

And, I thought, *if they didn't make it in time . . . well, at least I'd have the high ground. Maybe I could get Ann close to one of the cedars that grew on the uphill side of the playhouse rock.*

But how?

I'd tried herding Ann before—shoving her with my snout or shoulder. It didn't work. I had even grabbed her by the seat of her pants once or twice and tried to drag her away from danger. That didn't work, either.

My tail gave one little wag. There wasn't time for any more. Whining, I limped to Ann's side. I let out a little whimper. Just as I hoped, she hugged my neck.

"Poor Hoss. Did that mean old dog hurt you? Poor baby."

If she kept her grip around my neck, maybe I could take her to the big cedar—the one with branches low enough for her to get a hold of and climb. When the dogs got me down, when Ann was scared enough, maybe her instincts would take over. Maybe she would climb the tree, where she would be safe until Chrissy or Kevin found her.

We had to hurry.

I didn't look back until we reached the playhouse. I was afraid to. I didn't want to know how close the dogs were. When I turned to look, the yellow hound and the girl dog with the matted fur were sitting, as if waiting for something, at the edge of the cliff. I also saw a big black head, then strong shoulders, and finally a short, fat, stubby tail. As soon as the Rott pulled his massive body over the last rock, the other two rushed to him. They greeted and sniffed.

Then all three looked up the slope at us. Ann let go of my neck. I barked, then raced to the big tree. She didn't follow. Eyes wide, she stared at the three dogs. I barked again, louder this time. When she turned my direction, I balanced on my hind legs. With my front paws on a thick branch, I pretended to climb with my hind paws. It was kind of a surprise that they actually found a limb. With my hind paws now balanced on a branch, I reached with a front paw and pulled myself up. Then another limb.

Ann took a step toward me, then stopped. She turned, raised the little twig in her hand, and shook it. "You leave my Hoss alone. I'll paddle you good if you hurt him again."

Great! I thought. *I'm trying to get her to safety by climbing the tree. She's staying on the ground to protect me.*

I let go with my front paws, twisted, fell, and managed to land on all fours. I scampered to Ann's side. It took me only a second to find the dogs. They were about twenty yards below the playhouse. Instead of running, they closed the distance, slow and cautious. I guess they didn't quite know what to make of Ann. She was little, but her yelling and waving the floppy twig around . . . well, they just weren't sure why she wasn't trying to run away.

Confused or cautious—it didn't matter—they were still coming. It would just be a matter of time before they figured out that Ann was no threat.

I leaned against her. Let out my best whimper. When she didn't latch onto my neck, I whimpered three more times, trying to sound as pitiful as I could. Finally, she reached out to comfort me. With her hugging my neck, I managed to get her to the base of the tree before I heard a deep-throated growl.

I slipped into reverse, tugged my head free of Ann's grasp, and shoved her into the branches with my nose. I spun around.

Not more than ten feet away, the Rott stood directly in front of me. All of a sudden, the huge flat rock that my family called the playhouse seemed very small. He took a couple of steps to the left, sizing me up. Behind him, the girl dog with the grungy, matted coat appeared. She moved to my right. Just at the edge of my vision I saw the yellow dog. He was partially hidden beside a small cedar.

My lip curled past my gums. I felt my teeth grind inside my head. My growl was so deep, my chest shook.

The attack would come fast and furious. I

wasn't a huge cow with sharp hoofs. All three would rush me at once. When I turned to fight one, another would attack from the side. Another would hit when I tried to fight that one.

"Come on!" I growled. "What are you waiting for, you cowards. Come on!"

But inside my head, the truth wasn't as brave as my growl. Inside my head, I kept telling myself, *Don't go down. No matter how bad it hurts, don't go down. If you go down, then Ann . . . she's too little . . . she can't . . .*

Don't go down.

No matter what, don't go down!

Don't go down!

Chapter 17

The huge Rott charged. A half second later, the other two.

I expected the yellow dog to get to me first. I knew how fast he was. So I faced the Rott while watching the greyhound out of the corner of my eye. Sure enough, mouth open and running hard enough to plant those sharp teeth deep into my hide, he planned to knock me down.

At the last instant, I ducked my head and leaned back—the same move I'd used to get free from Ann's headlock.

He was going too fast to follow me. He turned his head as he flew past. His jaws snapped shut a fraction of an inch from my nose. With my head still low, I caught his back leg and bit down as hard as I could. He yelped, tumbled, and rolled sideways. I let go, but the force and speed of his charge spun me around. I managed to keep my balance and ended up facing the dog with the matted hair.

She snapped. Snarling and spinning in the other direction, I managed to escape her jaws and latch onto her neck. She yelped, just like the yellow dog. Only I didn't hurt her. Instead of getting a good hold, I managed only to yank a mouthful of matted fur and a couple of cockleburs out of her hide.

That gave me the split second I needed to hop to the side, keeping her between me and the Rott.

It was a good idea.

But it didn't work.

He plowed into her. She yelped and snapped at him. Her jaws grabbed nothing but air as the weight of his charge knocked her into me. Both of us tumbled. We landed on our backs, with her on top. She growled and bit—only she never got hold of me. I growled and bit, too—but her thick, matted hair kept me from getting anything but a mouthful of fuzz.

Looking up, I could see Ann. She was in the tree, but not high enough to be safe. Beyond her there was blue sky.

Get on your feet! My head screamed at me. *Get up quick. Give Ann a few more seconds.*

With all my might, I shoved with my front paws, squirmed and wiggled, trying to get out from under the thick carpet of matted hair. Finally, she rolled off. Quickly, I flipped on my side so I could get my feet under me.

The pain hit. My shoulder. My back.

I whined.

There was a black leg with a huge brown paw. The leg held my left shoulder down. The paw pressed on my chest. I caught the paw between my teeth and clamped down as hard as I could.

The Rott yelped, but the sound was muffled. By now he had trapped my left shoulder blade and part of my back between his massive jaws. As soon as I clamped onto his leg, I struggled to get up. He never loosened his hold—not even for a second. When the pain shot from my left leg, I yelped. Another dog was there, teeth chomping and slashing at the meaty part of my haunch.

The pain made my hold on that giant paw slacken enough for the Rott to yank it free. But before I could wiggle away, the paw slammed down again and pinned my head to the ground.

My right eye was pressed against the rock. I opened my left eye. I couldn't see Ann. I couldn't tell if she was safe. All I could see was the blue sky.

I couldn't get up. The massive weight was too much. I could hardly breathe.

Slowly, the Rott loosened his hold on my back

and shoulder. From the corner of my eye, I could see long sharp white teeth. His jaws were opened wide. I knew he was going for my throat.

I wiggled, struggled, fought to get up. But it was no use.

If only I had stayed on my feet, I thought. *If only I had fought longer, harder. Please let Ann be safe.*

I opened my eye again, hoping—no, praying—that I could see her safe, high up in the tree.

The only things I saw were white fangs and the blue of the sky.

Then . . . the blue sky turned black.

Chapter 18

No. Now the sky was blue.

No. It was black again.

What's going on? Am I dead already? I blinked. The color blue returned to the sky once more, but the huge sharp fangs weren't pointed at my neck. The Rott's mouth still gaped wide, but he was looking up instead of aiming at my throat.

And whoever had been gnawing on my leg was gone. It still hurt, but there were no teeth clamped into my flesh.

This is really weird, I thought. *Now the sky's turning black again. Not only black, but there's a tail dangling down from it. A long skinny tail with a tuft of hair on the end.*

Then . . . streaking through the sky like a bolt of lightning was a black shiny hoof.

There was a sudden jolt as the massive weight was lifted from my chest. I could breathe again. Panting, I gasped for air. It took me a second or two to get my bearings.

Struggling, I managed to get to my feet. My shoulder hurt like blazes, but I stayed up. Only trouble was, when I tried to turn and see what had just passed over me, my left hind leg gave way. Before my rump hit the ground, I did manage to twist far enough to see.

Tail swishing back and forth like an angry tomcat before a fight, Cookie moved toward the edge of the playhouse rock. The Rott stood there. He was still mad and ready to fight.

Growling and flashing those long white fangs of his, he circled to his right as Cookie neared. The calf was quick and strong, but he was also young and inexperienced.

I struggled to my feet again. My left hind leg wouldn't hold my weight, so I leaned on my right. I hopped on three legs, turning so Cookie could hear my bark.

"Watch him, Cookie! He'll try for your throat or nose!"

I'd only moved a hop or two toward them when a noise from behind turned me around.

Shaking and scared, Ann was climbing down from the tree. *Not now!* I thought.

Then, just a few feet from her, there was a movement. Hidden beneath the branches of the cedar on Ann's right was the yellow dog, who was crawling on his belly toward her.

The pain was still there, but all thought of it vanished when I saw my little Ann in danger. The yellow dog was almost out from under the branch nearest her when he saw me coming. His eyes bulged.

"Tried to chew my leg off, didn't you?" I snarled at him. "When I get a hold of you—"

He yelped—as loud as if I'd already bitten him—then scooted backward. Once clear of the limb where he was hiding, he took off down the hill.

"Get back here, you coward! Just let me get my jaws on you. I'll bite your tail off. I'll—"

It's kind of amazing how fast a scared dog can run, even one who's part greyhound. About halfway down the hill, he shot past the girl dog with the matted hair like she was standing still. Then she followed him across the pasture. Away from Tess. Away from Ann.

Hopping on three legs again, I turned back to Ann. Nudged her with my nose, trying to herd her once more up the cedar. It was no use. She just latched onto my neck and started crying. It hurt some, because she had her side pressed against the shoulder where the Rott's teeth had sunk in. But it was okay. At least I knew where she was, knew she was safe.

Safe?

Not if that Rott got away from Cookie and circled back.

I couldn't see with Ann's arm wrapped over me. I yelped when I put weight on my leg. Even then, I had to twist and wriggle my head from side to side until I could see out from under the sleeve of her pajamas.

Cookie stood straight and tall, keeping his nose out of the big dog's reach. Each time the Rott charged, Cookie would lift his front end off the ground and paw at him with his hooves. The dog always managed to dart away before those hooves came down. It seemed that neither one of them had the upper hand, and the battle might never end.

Until . . .

When I finally figured out what Cookie was doing, it made my tail wag—almost made me forget how bad my leg hurt. Maybe that little bull calf was smarter than I had given him credit for. Cookie wasn't trying to stomp him—he was *herding* him.

Each time the Rott dodged those hooves, Cookie would charge from the other direction. And each time it backed the dog closer and closer to the . . .

That's it, kid. I thought. *One more ought to—*

Cookie lowered his head and charged. But his charge was only one small short little hop. It worked. The big dog shuffled backward. Suddenly, his eyes flashed. He let out one little "Yip" as he disappeared over the edge of the playhouse rock.

There was considerable clunking, and crashing, and yelping—fact is, there was so much racket, it sounded like a landslide that might send the whole side of the slope down into the canyon.

Cookie stood there a moment, making sure the dog had no intention of trying to climb back up. Then he turned and rushed quickly to us. He leaned down and sniffed Ann, to make sure she was okay. Then he sniffed me.

"Are you all right?" he asked.

"Been better, but I'll make it." I noticed blood dripping from a cut on his nose. "How about you?"

"I'm fine." He swished his tail. "Wouldn't have been if you hadn't warned me. You barked a split second before he snapped at my nose. How did you know he was going to do that?"

"I've done it myself. Rex taught me how," I told him. "Kevin brought this crazy heifer home from an auction one time. She was wild as could be. Jumped clean out of the chute. She chased Kevin and had him cornered in the corral. The only way to stop her was to latch on to her nose. Soft nose. Heavy dog. That brought her down to her knees."

"Thank you, farm dog." Cookie snorted. "Pardon me—I meant to say, Thank you, *Hoss*."

"Thank *you*," I answered back. "That big guy had me. He was going for my throat. If you hadn't shown up when you did and kicked the stuffing out of him, well—"

"Hoss? Hoss? Where are you?"

The sound of Rex's bark made all three of us snap our heads around.

"Ann?" Chrissy called from behind him. "*Ann?* Where are you?"

"Mama? Mama, we're up here!" Ann called back. "Hoss and Cookie and me foughted off some really bad dogs. They were after a baby cow. They were bad, bad doggies. But we won."

Still holding me with one arm, Ann wrapped her other arm around Cookie's leg.

Panting and gasping for air, Rex scampered and stumbled onto the rock at the far side of the playhouse. He was so tired, he could hardly run, but he staggered over to us. "Smelled the dogs . . . smelled Ann . . . and you." He said between wheezes and coughs. "Went for help. Kevin . . . gone. Chrissy followed, but . . ." He stopped to pant and gasp. ". . . but not fast enough. Had to go back for her . . . twice."

With that he plopped on his rump. Ever so slowly he began to lean. When he was so far to one side that I thought he might tip over, I was glad I was there for him to lean on.

"You did great, Rex. Everything's okay. You brought help. That's the most important thing." I licked the side of his face. "Rest now. Catch your breath. It's all over. Nobody's hurt."

Chrissy raced toward us. All of a sudden, she stopped. Her mouth flopped open. Her eyes were almost as big around as her mouth, and her knees shook so hard, I just knew she was gonna drop at any second.

Chapter 19

"You're kidding," Tony said. "It scared you that bad?"

"Would have scared you, too." Chrissy's bangs bounced as she shot a blast of air up her forehead. "I wasn't even halfway across the playhouse rock, when I looked up and there's my baby with one arm wrapped around Hoss's neck and the other wrapped around that huge bull calf's leg. Her pajamas were soaked in blood."

"Shoot," Kevin interrupted. "There wasn't a scratch on her. And there was hardly any blood, either."

"Was too," Chrissy snapped.

"Just four or five drops from that cut on Cookie's nose. Maybe some from the gash on Hoss's shoulder," Kevin explained. "It looked like more 'cause it spread out when it soaked into her flannel pajamas. Did the same thing with the little blood spots on her side. Vet only gave Hoss six stitches and a round of antibiotics. There really wasn't that much blood—the way it soaked into the cloth just made it look like more."

The stitches weren't all that bad, I thought, as I listened to them. But remembering how Chrissy had pried my mouth open and stuck those nasty pills down my throat was enough to make me gag.

Chrissy folded her arms and leaned back in her chair. "Scared you too, Kevin. You just won't admit it."

"Okay. I'll admit it. When I got home from Mom and Dad's, Nicole told me that Ann was gone. When Rex came up and threw a total fit on the front porch, Chrissy followed him, figuring Ann was at the playhouse. That's where she was the last time. So Nicole and I hopped on the four-wheeler.

"They had just reached the bottom of the hill when we pulled up. And . . ." Kevin paused, leaning way forward. "I'll admit it scared the living daylights out of me. But I could tell real quick that Ann wasn't hurt. What worried me the most was seeing her hanging onto the leg of that doggone calf."

"I wasn't scared," Nicole boasted. She rocked back in her chair like her mother. "I knew Ann was sneaking—"

"You knew?" Chrissy shrieked. "You knew and you didn't tell us?"

Nicole flinched. Then she gave her mother a half-hearted smile and shrugged. "I didn't know she was sneaking off to the playhouse. I did know she was sneaking out to the corral to pet Cookie. I heard her get up one morning, and I watched her. I wasn't scared, because she was staying close to the house. And because I knew Cookie wouldn't hurt her."

Kevin had just taken a sip of his coffee. He acted like he was going to choke. I was glad he had time to spit it back into his cup instead of spraying the whole kitchen. When he caught his breath, he smiled. "Nicole wasn't scared. The second she saw her little sister, she started screaming. Thought she was gonna bust my eardrum."

I nudged Rex with my nose. "Nicole knew. Did you know about Ann petting Cookie, too?"

"Yep," Rex nodded.

"I'm the watchdog. How could I have missed that?"

Rex shrugged his ears. "Well . . . ah . . . well, she usually sneaked out of the house while you were off on your Daybreak Patrol. Got back inside before you returned, I guess."

"How's old Hoss doing?" Tony looked over his shoulder to where I was curled up near the door.

Everybody looking at me made my tail thump the floor.

"Vet took the stitches out the day before yesterday," Kevin said.

Tony turned in his chair and leaned back to scratch my head. "Looks like Hoss is good as new."

My tail thumped the floor again. *I feel great. Even told Rex I'd help him ambush rabbits tonight.*

Tony turned back to the table. He leaned way to the side, so he could see out the kitchen window. "I still can't believe it. I mean, I can see them from here. See them with my own eyes. Little Ann's standing out in the pasture, and that big calf's leaned down so she can scratch his forehead and behind his ears. He looked like he'd make you a good bull. But wild as he was, I didn't think he'd ever calm down. I wonder what Ann did—how she turned a bull-headed, wild crazy calf into a . . . well, a family pet."

My head snapped up from the cool floor. Ears perked, my tail slapped the tile.

"I know! I know!"

Then I realized that no matter how hard I tried—how much I said with the movement of my ears, twitching my whiskers, wiggling my eyes, or giving off my different smells—my people would *never* understand me.

Truth of the matter was, Ann was nice to him. That's how Cookie explained it when I asked him. He confessed that he was scared when they moved him and his mother to a new place. He reminded me that, when he first got here, Tony and Kevin beat on the trailer. That scared him even more. Then they poked at him with a big metal bar. That made him mad. When he came out of the trailer, Chrissy and Nicole waved their arms at him and yelled. I chased him—barked and snapped at his heels.

Ann didn't do anything to him. She just looked sad, because she knew he was so scared. From what she said with her eyes, Cookie knew Ann felt sorry for him and wanted to be his friend.

And I knew Cookie would never hurt her. No matter what.

Tony made a grunting sound as he got up from his chair. "Guess we'd better go work those cattle. You gonna work the little bull calf first?"

Kevin got up from his chair. "Already have."

"How'd you get him into the chute?" Tony asked. But before Kevin could answer, Tony started shaking his head and waving both hands. "Never mind. Don't tell me. Ann led him in there for you."

Kevin smiled. "Nope. Gave him his shots, poured the fly repellant and insecticide on his back, and clipped the ear tag in—right out in the field. Ann didn't have to lead him anyplace. She just stood there and held onto his leg."

All Tony could do was shake his head.

I followed them outside, and as they talked, I finally heard what I'd been waiting for!

Fact is, I really knew it all along. But I had to hear it—had to hear the words from Kevin's mouth before I could tell Cookie.

My shoulder was still a little sore, but it didn't slow me down. I took off like a shot for the field. Ann met me just this side of the fence. She was headed inside to help Chrissy and Nicole start dinner for Tony, Kevin, and the other two men who were coming to help with the herd. I stopped long enough for her to pet me, licked her hand, then tore off again.

"It's official," I barked, sliding to a stop in front of my friend. "You *are* the herd bull!"

Cookie was glad.

That evening, when I told Rex, he was glad, too. "I think he'll make a good one. Ought to make your job a little easier, with him taking care of the cows." Then with a wag of his tail, he added. "Ought to make my job easier, too. With him around, you won't have to check the herd so often. Give you more time to help me with those pesky rabbits."

Rex hid at his corner of Chrissy's flower garden. I hid behind the bush sunflower on my side. All was quiet and peaceful.

To be honest, it was the first time in weeks that I had felt so relaxed.

Just after dark, my head started to feel heavy. It bobbed, and I jerked it back up a couple of times. I finally rested my chin on my paws. My eyes felt heavy, too. I could rest them for a few minutes and still hop to my feet if Rex chased a rabbit this way. So I let them close. But just for a second or two.